EVERY BODY LOOKING

CANDICE ILOH

Dutton Books

DUTTON BOOKS
An imprint of Penguin Random House LLC, New York

Copyright © 2020 by Candice Iloh

Dutton is a registered trademark of Penguin Random House LLC.

Visit us online at penguinrandomhouse.com

Library of Congress Cataloging-in-Publication Data is available.

Printed in the United States of America

ISBN 9780525556206

10 9 8 7 6 5 4 3 2 1

Design by Anna Booth
Text set in Plantin MT Pro

For all my wondering, questioning,
and dreaming little sisters/sibs feeling your way
through everything so you can be and do what you want
in this world. For the first-gen kids. For the young queers.
For the dancers and wannabe dancers. For the survivors.
For all of us who needed to change our mind.
For baby Me.

EVERY BODY LOOKING

GRADUATION DAY

Just look at me
they got me out here
wearing a dress
heels
makeup

hope Mama's proud

she sure does look like it
looking at me and squealing
like proud mamas do when
their baby looks something

like she came from them

her squeals bounce
from every wall of this hotel lobby
her screams shake from
her fragile body exploding

like she's shocked by her own joy

unsteady heels click
against the tile toward the person she can say
was the best thing she ever did
with her life

Here's the scene: I'm seventeen and graduating
from high school
and this weekend I learn to juggle

my father and his new wife
are on their way to the Home of the Chicago Doves

decked out, like they're about to glide down the church's red carpet
him in his crispiest suit, her bulging from a flowered dress

my baby brother dressed
as Dad's mini identical twin

belted in the back seat
of my father's golden Toyota Camry

is giddy knowing nothing
about what day it is

or how his big sister
will survive it

after picking up her own mommy
keeping her seated somewhere

she can fidget
far from his side of the family

Mama fidgets
in my passenger seat
more on edge than me
maybe cause it's been
like five years since we've seen
each other but she is here

scoffs under her breath
thinking, just like her
this hoopty is proof
of yet another thing
I don't need

shrugs away small thoughts
not knowing
Dad demanded
I save and buy my first Camry
myself

sits and tugs
at her lopsided wig
pulls down the mirror
reapplies bloodred lipstick
smudges some on her cheeks
with her fingers

and I thank god knowing
without this
I may not
recognize her

We pull into my high school's parking lot
for the last day I will ever have to smile at these people like I
ever belonged here / for the ten minutes it takes Mama and
me to get to the stands along the football field, a place she
has never seen / I imagine the sounds of our heels to be / like
a song we are for once dancing to together / today / I'm not
angry / at her slurred speech / I'm not angry / at her missing
teeth / I'm not angry / at her fuss / I'm not angry / that she
looks nothing like / the last time I saw her / or that / I don't
know when the next time will be / for the ten minutes it takes
Mama and me to get to the stands along the football field / I'm
just happy we're both here / alive

My name is Ad*a*
but not really
it's what my father's side
calls me cause I was born

first

and on this day
I'm only three months
from leaving this place behind

they tell me there's
a big world out there
and they tell me

there's so much I can do
and I know nothing
but this city

but my father
but these schools
where I've always

been one of few specks
of dingy brown
in a sea of perfect white

but I know the bible
and I know how to do

the right things

so how hard could college
really be

How hard could it be to

1. Find a dress that both Mama and Dad would like.
2. Make sure the dress was loose enough to hide all my heavy.
3. Put on heels I could stand for more than three hours.
4. Pick Mama up in my own car.
5. Get Mama to my soon-to-be old school.
6. Sit Mama somewhere I could see her.
7. Run back and forth between Mama and Dad.
8. Smile for every camera.
9. Smile with Mama.
10. Smile when Mama insists that she be the first, after it's over, to have dinner with me.

Dad smiles for his final picture with me
loosening the awkward grip
tightly held on the outside
of my right arm

his sharp signature cologne
left to linger across
my shoulders

a scent just as strong
as the bass
in the shifting tone of his voice

proud of you, kid
you did good
he says

as if I'd done
my entire high school bid
just now, all in one day

thanks, Dad
I smile back, bashful
warm under the way

he looks at me
on the days
I do right

standing back I look
at the softness peeking through
thick folds of my father's face

watch yet another attempt

to pull his belted suit pants
over the bottom of his round belly

now at the end of a long day
under the football field sun with beads of sweat
faithfully dabbed across his widow's peak

by an old white cloth always tucked
in his back pocket basking in the praise
of his job well done

After the pictures are done
caught back and forth
on opposite sides
of the crowded field

buzzing with families proud
of children
they don't really know

we pull into the driveway
as the sky surrounding Dad's house
is deepening toward black from gray

Mama glances toward
his front door and back
toward the road behind us

scared

I think to place a hand
on her trembling shoulder
but settle for telling her *it's okay, Mom*

tell her *we'll be a minute*
tell her *I just need to change*
tell her *they're not home yet*

but Dad's house is my house too

Mama looks back at me
wanting too much

to see where I live
but too proud to admit
she needs my permission

stares into the side of my face
hungry for any scrap
I might drop for her to catch

reaches for my hand
as I lift it just in time
from the gear stick for her to miss

shifting my foot
from the brake pedal
checking my phone for the time

I tell Mama
we've got thirty minutes
before my father and that woman

come home

Some kids grew up coming home
to the smell of mustard greens
special recipe mac and cheese
cornbread from scratch and cookies
baking in the oven

to the sound of their mama
screamin at somebody on the tv
getting on her nerves for the tenth time
while she watches the same shows

announcing to the whole house
that *this will be*
the last time I trip
over a child's raggedy school shoes

or telling them *you better*
clean up that funky alleyway
that you like to call
your bedroom

some kids grew up
being asked about
why their grades ain't
better than that and fussin
over homework they need to do

but my mama
was different
my mama just
wasn't really   the type

To keep tabs on me like that
wasn't really my mama's style I learned years ago
when she started asking me my age

I'd look back at her and wonder
how she could forget when she had me

how she could push out a whole person
and just forget

Mama and I both forget
about time the minute I turn the key
unlocking the front door to Dad's house

suddenly it's like we're surrounded
by a museum of forbidden family

knowing she can look but not touch
Mama is everywhere her feet

take her wanting to see what we've
been up to while she's away

the walls covered with me at every age
that she struggles to remember

Mama getting lost in all the picture frames
my fancy life of birthday parties and school plays

my first dance recital on a park stage
dressed in colorful West African cloth like the other girls

a buzz from my phone reminds me
to get her upstairs so I can change my clothes

From upstairs I can hear Dad's car door slam
and I know they are home already
Mama's fidgets come back again
and I'm angry
when just seconds ago
her soft hands were gliding
across my pictures
my clothes
my animals
stuffed with love
and a pillow with her picture
stuck inside its plastic cover frame

freshly painted red fingernails
touching just about everything
happy to be in the room
where her child sleeps
happy to be inside
and here she is
now filled with fear
filled with how they will see her
a stranger squatting
in her own daughter's
bedroom

I run from my room
closing the door behind me /
down the stairs / I run / so I can
smile and twirl / real sweet once more /
for Dad / and his new wife
to dance / in their still-fresh
pride of the new high school graduate

where is she, Dad asks

I tell him
she is upstairs
tell him
we'll only be a few minutes
tell him
this is my house too

his new wife looks and sucks her teeth
upstairs, one of the first, down here the last
my baby brother off playing and oblivious
and suddenly I know somewhere
it's written, somewhere it says
my mama shouldn't be here

Mama shouldn't be here
so we're gone quick and quiet five minutes later to eat
anywhere but here and Mama is cussin but I smile and turn
on the radio, blast the ac cause it's just her and me

I ask her where she wants to go and she tells me *anywhere girl*
I'm with my baby
I knew we shouldn't have gone in there! chile, did you see how she
was lookin

I pretend it's all nothing and drive us to my favorite restaurant
thumping my fingers
on my lap to the beat, leave Mama to keep talking and talking
to the tune of herself

She already answered this herself
when I come back to the motel for her the next day
a question she asks in the car on the way
to my graduation party and it sounds like some
kind of silly joke where she's playing or must have
forgotten the party where we are headed is for me

> *I don't really feel*
> *like bein bothered*
> *with all them people*
> *all them people I don't know*
> *and they just gon be*
> *lookin at me and I'm just gon be*
> *sittin by myself and I just ain't*
> *in the mood to be bothered, you know*

I ask her what she wants to do instead
but tell her I'm going to my party, after all
it was thrown for me, it's either she comes
or she gets on the next train back, cause
today is supposed to be about me

> *oh I don't know but*
> *I don't feel like bein bothered*
> *I really ain't tryna go to no party*

she says

Away from the party on this drive to the train station
it's only silent for a few minutes
before I'm called every name

I'm sure I'm not supposed to be
called by my mama but I know

this is how she says she's angry
this is how she says this is her day too

this is how she says she's sorry
in her own way, as a mother

for breaking all the rules

The first thing I do after everyone is gone
is shut the door
close the blinds

sometimes being dramatic
is my thing but

this really was
the first time I've seen

this much cash
ever

the room I'd slept in
for the past seven years

painted a Pepto-Bismol pink
was now marked

an old green
at the center

I'd opened each
graduation card alone

skipped Hallmark notes
telling me *Good Job!* and *Great Things Ahead!*

skipped every *Congrats on your big day!*
in search of what mattered most

told Dad I didn't feel like
being mushy

in front of all
those people

but truth is
I just wanted

to count my money
in peace

Dad says having money brings peace
always quotes what seems like
his favorite bible verse that
says money is the answer
to everything

money answereth to all matters
he says so seriously whenever
we talk about dreams or just
pulling into a gas station

I know you think
all I care about is money
but you can't tell me life isn't easier
when you have extra in your pockets

bible verses and African proverbs
always being the half answers
to my questioning
but looking down into the pile

this time, maybe he's right

Right now
I've got about a thousand dollars
and two months until I'm officially on my own
a stack of bills in my hand, gifts
from Dad's friends, names and faces
I couldn't remember but Dad told them
come

said *the people that really love you*
will bring you things, shower you
with gifts if they really care about you
come to your party with thick envelopes
never show up with
empty hands

My hands hold
more money now
than I've ever seen
all at once

so I slowly
count it all
again and again

passing dirty paper
through moistening fingers
wondering what it means

imaging what
all this green can do
hundreds of miles away

there's no way
I can tell him
how much I really have

there's no way
I could tell him
without him making

demands

The next morning I trash the empty envelopes
stand still in my half-empty bedroom
in the silence of this empty house
wishing I was already gone

two months ago Dad took me
to visit my new college
and my mind is already gone

wonder what would happen
if Dad and his new wife came
back from the store and my body was already

gone

I am gone again
before Dad has the chance
to come knocking at my door after
everyone is back from church to ask me
how much or if I made sure to say *thank you*
to all of his friends who put something
in my hand

I roll down my windows
letting the highway air cool my thoughts
allowing the rough wind to pull all the questions
from shoulders and neck
turn the music up louder
cause it's just me

text Dad to let him know I had to work
tell him I took an extra shift for college money
that I forgot to tell him and not to worry
that I realize it's graduation weekend
that it's no big deal because I know
everyone will be in bed early

knowing when I get back
from dance class
no one will notice the sweat
no one will question me
tiredly raiding the kitchen
and Dad will be in his room
pretending to sleep

Dad didn't know much about when I worked
after I got my car and I was always busy
if he knew I was still taking all these dance classes
he'd think I was wasting precious money and my time

rolling and shaking to djembe and afrobeats
sometimes accompanied by live drums
the way we were taught

to listen for the rhythm
to listen for the break
to follow and to lead

sometimes they would have me dance
facing the drummers following hands
that spoke to our steady feet

smiling at their own hands
pleased by the room's energy
playing while our bodies flew free

At age four dance hadn't been free
but it was a cheaper way for Dad
to teach me about where we came from
barefoot we danced bellies out wrapped in
colorful fabric skirts and dresses
made in our home country

every saturday Dad would take me
for my history lesson where I'd learn
Yoruba and Igbo songs the teacher would sing
for us while giving us moves
to travel across the floor

when we didn't have the money to travel overseas
learned rhythms to tell stories
learned steps used to ground us
began learning how to find home later on
in my own skin

When you get too big to be carried
when you start wanting things
beyond food
or a place to sleep

when you start needing
a way to make sense
of everything happening

when you start growing
further away from
what used to be home

you go looking for somewhere
that lets you be
what's inside your head

you go find a way to get back
to your own history lesson
to your own way of being alive

How can I tell Dad
about what makes me feel most alive
when since I've been born his whole existence
has been sacrificed for me?

what can I tell him when his every breath
has been about keeping me safe
and teaching me to do what's right?

how can I tell someone who does nothing
before he has a chance to pray
that the god I'm getting to know teaches me

how to seek my own face?

He will not understand the way I feel
every time I get to dance
is the opposite of it all

that when I tell my body to move
it can

when I tell my body to feel
it can

when I tell my body to stretch
it can

when I tell my body to try
it can

and every time
I go a little further

and every time
I learn my body is mine

and every time
I learn my body's wishes

are my command

SUMMER BEFORE COLLEGE

And I command satan to flee
from every space Ada will travel on this new path
and I command every negative spirit to be loosed
and I pray Ada will continue to obey
your voice, oh lord

her body might tell her to hang with bad people
she will not go

her body might tell her to go to the clubs
she will not go

her body might tempt her to dress sexy
she will not do it, lord

because she is a child of god
submitted to your will
created for your glory

so lord I pray as Ada leaves this morning
that you cover her in your blood
walk for her
speak for her
breathe for her
when she doesn't know what to do

and help her be a light to the other students
so at the end of the year she brings
more faithful servants to you, lord

in Jesus name
amen

Dad squeezes my hand and I know I will not miss
these prayers in someone else's name
these requests that god stop me
these scriptures written by men
these memories that no one knows about

where I never
got to decide

maybe leaving this place
maybe choosing no longer to hide
will set me free

one day

Dad no longer needs to know all my plans
as we pack his car to head to the airport
he's still talking about god's will

this is how I know Dad is scared
I'm moving to a whole new state

where he won't be able to watch over me
where he won't know the people I'll be around

this means I'll have to trust my Self
he's releasing my Self to the world

but happy knowing I'll
study in his footsteps   as far as he knows

that one day
I'll make a whole lot of money

that prayer and money
will keep my Self safe

Safety (safe·ty)
/'sāftē/
noun
the condition
of being protected from
or unlikely to cause danger
risk
or injury

as in
to ensure
our safety
Dad clasps
his hands
around mine
having us
bow our heads
at our seats
just after boarding
the flight

as in
to ensure
his safety
Dad thumbs warning cards
he's seen tucked behind seats
hundreds of times
while flight attendants
tell us what to do
like this
was our first time
flying

as in

for my own

safety

Dad reminds me

that I'm not flying

697 miles away from home

to be like this world

I should remember

from the moment

I set foot on campus

I'm supposed to be

a light   for Christ

The lights dim

through the cabin once we're off ground // Dad crushes a
pack of peanuts and a drink before falling asleep beside me
// outside my window is all sky while clouds float far beneath
// I'm thinking this is what it's like when you're too far above
everything for regular life to matter // that old life in Chicago
where I was my old me // everyone telling me about this new
person I'll be while begging me not to change at the same time
// new city new people but always new in Christ // youth pastor
always teaching how god transforms us by washing us clean //
I am wondering about this new feeling god might give me far
from hands once laid on me // what church what choir what
pew awaits to remind me whose I am // and who am I without
all these reminders back in my old city // this charge feeling
like the heavy of my carry-on packed with // notebooks my
laptop two bibles and my freshmen welcome guide

to college

When people talk about college
they never really talk about
how you're going to
change before
your whole family's eyes

and they're not
going to be happy about it
instead
they'll ask you

what's that thing in your nose?
where'd you get those words from?
have you forgotten how to call home?

when's the last time
you prayed, huh?

I didn't have to think to pray
before I ate, I would just do it
before I laid down for the night
before I got into a stranger's car
before the car would pull off
before I walked down the street at night
before I walked down the street in the morning
before an exam
before an exam I didn't study for

because that's what we did back home
I didn't study much at first
I never had to before
cause I didn't know how
it was new to me
like this freedom
like this new city
like this new bed
like this own mind
so this own body
decided to sleep in
this time
when sunday came

When the first Sunday away came around
I learned there was a shuttle
and the shuttle was for anyone
who wanted to

remember their religion
cause ain't no reason you gotta
backslide just cause you're in college

if not now, when else would you
need JEEZUS more?

the shuttle would take us
to Zion Church of Christ at
nine o'clock and if you weren't
there somebody would know
and if you were there somebody
would know
and you would get a special hug
if you came wearing the
scent of last night's party, body
smelling of perfume and sweat
mascara running laps around
your eyelids

your shirt loose enough now
to cut a step for the lord
your neck fighting to lift back up
after bowing
to pray

Growing up my dad would pray
before during and after
everything and honestly
it was cool until it made us
late for things
and made me question
why we couldn't do things
with our own strength

started wondering what
my father was so afraid of
what was on the other side
of amen
that was so bad
we couldn't just
do it

MIDDLE SCHOOL

A week into the sixth grade Dad says
we're trying a new church
says he's been praying
to the lord for a new home

this is the third church
in three weeks and I

am just praying
for my first real friends

We can see this new church
from almost a mile up the street
the building is half the size
of its enormous parking lot, several cars
spilling onto the roads lining what
seems to be the entire neighborhood
a large sign is dug deep into the church's front lawn
large black letters say that us that have fallen far   from god
can still be welcomed here

Dad begins to say *wow*
begins to say *my god*
begins to say *thank you Jesus*
under his breath but just enough
for me to hear

I'm wondering, when we park,
how long it'll take
to get inside

To get inside
after making the pilgrimage
through the parking lot we enter
the two doors that open themselves
when you step on the sensing carpets
the ushers are at the doors then in the hallway
then in the second set of hallways serving us all the
*god bless you*s and *hallelujah*s and *my lord*s that we can get
I am sure my father is impressed at the shine of their gleaming teeth
and matching suits, the swing of their hands raising to clap
and sing politely
one leads us through the double doors to seats to the far left
before the choir, diagonal
from us the pastor and first lady are sitting, I hear another *my
lord* another *thank you Jesus*

and I know we are here to stay

It's clear we'll stay here
watching Dad take in the plush burgundy seats
at least one hundred rows of brown skin cloaked in tailored
    dress
clapping perfectly manicured hands
jumping and stomping their feet
under the spell of the finest full choir
drums and most impressive organ

the congregation crying out in unison
while the praise team leads song after song
Dad entranced as the pastor nods approvingly
from the front row, bobbing his head
one hand resting on the lap of his first lady

the whole flock shines in collective *yes*
everyone's best jewelry gleaming
a flood of hands outstretched
each one a sign of surrender
each one a bowed head, a shed tear   or a bended knee

The pastor rises to lead
the choir in the pre-tithing selection
before he asks the congregation for
ten percent of their earnings
he sings with us a song that creates
all the tears

what I hear is that Jesus loves me
and how we all know this because the bible
tells us so and I know that is good
I know that it's good we're going
off of what the bible says
more than anything
Dad said we needed to
find a home where they teach the
Word of God

I had never questioned
how the bible
was the Word
of God
when many
of the books
were written
by men
whose names
sounded American

apparently
Matthew
Mark
Luke
John
Timothy
James
Peter
Paul
are
the Words
of God

Words are powerful
unless they're not biblical
unless they're not written by men
unless they're unlike
Jesus's spit itself

why can't I pray outside of his name?
why is my name not enough?

The pastor sits for the choir's last song
before he shares with us
the Word of God, and
several women come
floating out from
doors just next to the band
dressed in gold bodysuits
with purple dresses
gently covering their curves
but accenting the way
their bodies fly
to the rhythm across the marble
floors in praise but
really it's possession
taking over them
catching some type of spirit
that tells me something inside
knows how to control this
they know
why they move, how they
lift their feet, how they
bend their backs
how this dance
is their own
the *something greater*
in their thighs, in the rush
of their blood
and they are looking
to the sky
to their hands
to themselves smiling
and suddenly my face
is wet and I can see
myself up there, near them too

Dad catches me like this
lifts one eyebrow
but still
thinks it's the Holy Ghost
that got me
thinks this is something
other than seeing
my own reflection

After service

I stare at my reflection in the bathroom / see myself / twirl one
time / see myself / lift my eyes to the hills / the hills are my
hands / see myself / flick my wrists slow / see myself / thrust
my chest forward like I am pushing something away / see
myself laugh at this silly girl thinking she can point toe and dip
and move like that / see myself wanting to master my body /
like the dancers

The dancers were the last
things on Dad's mind
instead he asks me for my notes

this is how he monitors if I was paying
attention to what the pastor said we should do

to be better followers of the Christ, Our Lord
I hand them over proudly, knowing how to be

a good student, knowing how to be
a good follower, knowing these

are not my own words
anyone can find

and use to
expose me

On this night the stillness of my bedsheets
allows me to daydream
about the dancers in ways
I could not see them
moving their feet across
the church altar floor
their angelic bodies
leaping and stretching
twirling to a tune
meant for god
and still I see
their eyes looking
at each other

My eyelids don't seem able to meet each other
so tonight
quietly I climb out of bed

walk in short steps toward my desk
and reach for the top drawer hoping

it makes no creaks, no sound to
alert my father that his child is not asleep

I am lucky when the drawer that holds my things
comes sliding out, and I reach

for one sheet of paper, a pencil and
to the small switch of my lamp

I begin
with her feet

For her toes
my pencil draws
a short
curved
line
down
toward
the bottom
of the
page
and
rounds
just
where
they meet
the ground
then swoops
back up
to the arch
of her
balancing
feet, on
pointe
just like
a pro

But what pro takes this long
to get it
right

since I can't sleep
tonight

I'm going back
for another

and another
sheet

with each jagged line
with each draft

going back
trying to see

my pointed toe dancer
just as she's kept

appearing
in my dreams

I am sketching and shading
the way we were taught in art class
to make something look real

how they taught us
to use our fingers for smudging the lead
to blend

how they taught us
to use the tip of the pencil for thin marks
to define

how they taught us
to observe something
we want to bring to life

how they taught us
to use the pink eraser only if we wanted
to forget

our mistakes

I make the mistake
of forgetting about the time
and hours later it is morning

Dad finds me nestled
on my bedroom carpet

laid out
on top of every page

where her feet are
drawn too many times

for me to count
each sketch proof

of two things
I'm not good at

each sketch
a reason
that I'll be late

You want to be grown
but you can't even
wake up for your alarm

you want to be grown

but you can't even
sleep like a proper human being

you want to be grown

but you spend the whole night
drawing this silly thing

Dad bends
down to reach the closest copy
of the silly thing

releases a dramatic sound
as he curves over

his bulging belly
and just looks

one eyebrow lifts, shoots
another look, his forehead rippling

into curves of both suspicion and
confusion, drops the silly thing

my eyes watching it float
to the floor

and says
you have
five minutes to
get ready

I'm ready
in ten minutes
or something like that
meet Dad in the
driveway where the engine is running
for effect even though he was
threatening that by now he
would have left me

I scoot into the back seat
our eyes meeting in the rearview
after the rush, my heart pounding
through my t-shirt

his hands let go of the steering wheel
and move to his lap as he utters

let us pray

And father god protect Ada from distraction
he prays

keep her ears and eyes open
he prays

cover her with your blood
cleanse her
of the spirit of disobedience
help her stay focused, lord
he prays

thank you for your loving mercy
for letting us see another day
in Jesus name   amen

Dad clears his throat
lifts his head from prayer
this man of unyielding faith
meeting my eyes again
in the rearview mirror
a paused silent protest
against my ride to school

waiting for me to agree
so I too say

amen

COLLEGE

The first week is supposed to be anything but serious
so I take my new roommate's advice
decide to go out and wander with her on campus

we take the stairs down avoiding all the families still here
crowding old dingy elevators that go out of service every hour

grab the maps and lists of places
to spend our money from the dorm front desk

stand briefly outside watching rental cars pull away
thankful dad didn't linger like a lot of them did

make our way on campus
to find the food

Feels like it takes the whole four years
we'll be here to get on main campus
where we find everyone and everything

flocks of college boys stopping my roommate
every five minutes to holler and asking

yo, where you from, sweetheart? and *can I call you sometime?*
where you stay at, shorty? damn, I'm tryna study with you, tho

able to smell the freshmen meat instantly
rushing at the sight of the overly glossed lips

and shine of her cell phone she'd blinged
her body a magnet for all who wanted a taste

Watching her lick her lips as if she could taste
the cherry in her cheap lip gloss
tossing her hand out like flyers
I watched her handle all potential
players and these questions
like a pro

Sophia wit' a p-h
save it right
I don't spell it
like them other bitches out here

says

I'm from BROOKLYN
repeating for the fifth boy
leaning into the *OOK*
with more attitude
than anyone needs

says

oh, and this is my roommate
y'all don't be rude,
an instruction given with a twist
of her body making coy eye contact
with each boy now in her immediate vicinity

yeah that's what I heard her
daddy call her
she African
she say the A *different, y'all*

says this
glancing at me with a smile
flinging another wink

After like the tenth boy I leave
Sophia to her crowd of admirers
keep walking to the cafeteria alone
now feeling my stomach grumbling

wonder if I look as lost as I am
follow the groups that look
as young and dumb as me

find it and suddenly
feel like I'm back
in high school

sort of

Except here everybody's black
or
brown
and I'm not the only one
who looks like their parents
gave them a name not everyone

can pronounce

Ada (Aah-dah!)
in the Igbo
language

means *first daughter*

means oldest girl

means pressure

means *you are expected*

to do a lot of things
you don't want to do
because the honor
of this family

rests on your back

Back in high school
everyone hated the days
you had to find somewhere new to sit

when you had to find somewhere you fit
and wouldn't be cast off like these

crusty options they're serving
in this massive bootleg food court

here you've got so-called choices
if you have a taste for their versions

of Italian, Chinese, or Indian
and when that fails

there's always days-old salad
a sad sandwich bar, stale Cap'n Crunch

or good old mac and cheese

I didn't walk around with a cheesy smile
searching for friends
or for anyone who'd take me in
at their table
in high school
so college wasn't different

made a circle through the crowd
got in a random line where
the lady slapped some rice and
a random brown stew on my plate
found a seat somewhere to inhale it

by myself

When sitting by yourself
eating food
that doesn't
taste like
home you
eat fast
and leave
without being
noticed

SIXTH GRADE

The sixth grade is a strange time.
There are suddenly big tests and first dances and health
classes where the teacher is suddenly asking you to watch
a vagina expand because a baby is coming out of it and
suddenly you need to know about this and the bell rings and
you change classrooms and are given four minutes to get to
your next one. All kinds of things happen in the hallway as
you move to the next one. You hear and see everything and
sometimes it's about you. Sometimes everyone is talking about
or laughing at you and you don't really have time to be sure
because you can't be late and you don't really have time to cry.
Your father says these people are not important. That when
you leave this place you will forget all about them and they will
be nobody and whether or not they thought your hair was the
most hilarious thing or your voice was too deep or that your
mustache was visible on this day will not matter. They will not
matter. Crying is stupid when it is over a boy or the group of
girls who you just wanted to like you enough to make you their
friend.

I discovered sixth grade also meant real freedom

when I learned

now I can run the house by myself

now there are hours between

getting out of school and Dad's car

pulling into the driveway

in these hours

I drop my bookbag

in the middle of the kitchen floor

I eat everything

I want from the fridge

I walk over

to Dad's massive speaker

flip the switch to radio

turn the volume up high

and pretend the living room is mine

and for once

I am the chosen one

picked first for the stage

The living room became my perfect stage
every weekday afternoon
with its wide space &
with its loud speakers &
with its bass that trembled
so deep
it pissed off
the neighbors

I didn't think about the neighbors
until day three
of my solo performance sessions
rounding my back and
moving my legs to the beat
across our living room
carpet when
I hear the front
doorbell ring
and on the other side
of the door

there's no applause

just two cops
who'd come
to shut me down

As I stand on the inside of our front door
and lift my hand
to reach the golden knob
my eyes trace its round
and shining surface

they bounce back
and forth between
its gleam and the tremble
of curved fingers

and I hear the boom
of Dad's voice
wonder if when he

warned me about strangers
he also meant the police

My still-trembling fingers
finally grasp the knob
as I take one last look
out through the peephole
past their white faces
and onto the street

I turn it
force a smile
say nothing

Nothing is wrong except
there is a car with sirens on its roof in our driveway&
there are two tall white men standing on our porch&
there are two men looking beyond me into our kitchen&
there are neighbors peeking out windows at our house&
there are huge cops with guns I can see who've come to tell me

that I'm too loud
too much
too free

After I've closed the door behind me
and they've driven off
having warned me
I've already told myself
that I will not tell Dad
he doesn't need to know
they'd been here
he doesn't need to know
the neighbors were looking
he doesn't need to know
for a moment in the space between the officers and myself

there was nothing to protect me

Dad works in mysterious ways to protect me
we pull into the middle school parking lot / he announces
that Aunty is coming / followed by *have a good day* / he liked
dropping bombs and leaving / no time for discussion / no
debate / so I spend all eight periods thinking about how /
Aunty is coming with her big suitcase / Aunty is coming with
her big suitcase full of shoes and stockfish / her big suitcase
full of gifts and egusi / her big suitcase full of photos and fanta
orange / just as I am growing used to being alone and in our
big house / Dad tells me Aunty is coming from Nigeria to our
house / to live

Forever?

> *She is just coming for a visit*
> Dad says

But you said—

> *What does it matter?*
> Dad asks

But what about my cousins
I ask

> *They are coming too*
> Dad says

But what about Uncle
I ask

> *He's not coming this time*
> *someone's got to watch their house*

I don't know why
their big Nigerian house
needs to be watched but
by the hard waves crashing
against my dad's forehead
I know not to ask

I don't care much anyway

my baby cousins are coming
Aunty is coming
though I'll soon have to start sharing
all this space   once all mine
I can't wait to see

what my favorite aunty brought
from where Dad calls *home*

Aunty's arrival brings every new thing
only five days after Dad tells me
so we're cleaning all the rooms
rearranging everything
I am thinking
about what
it'll be like

to be the oldest
of three

Friday morning I learn
being the oldest means Aunty and cousins take my bed and
what remains are my purple-and-pink blanket two pillows
and me left to learn how to sleep above old carpeting like a
camping adventure on this second floor of our suburban house
and I will learn how to sleep with my face to the ground with
my bed in the next room and my favorite dresser emptied so
this house can fit us all

Aunty thanks god in the doorway
and greets me with a smile
and long sucking of her teeth

ah-ah! Ada, baby
you have grown so much
I see you have been eating well-well
was di news, baby

Aunty's pidgin English
is so cool
I'm almost
able to ignore
that she
has already
called me
fat

I rush to hug her
catch the familiar
whiff of Nigerian sweat
in the pocket of her neck
where she holds me

I can forgive it
knowing she has
been on a plane
for fourteen hours

with a toddler
a baby
and stockfish

The first time Aunty cooked stockfish in our house
I didn't know // the stench would become like // catching a
whiff of a girl in desperate need of a shower // probably two
days into her period // the scent clinging to me too fishy and
rank // the kind of scent // they say to look out for // a sign
you've messed up // your body's natural pH wearing panties
too tight // or being too fast for your age // but stockfish //
dried and hard // is a loved ingredient found in tons of Igbo
dishes // tastes much better than it smells // sticks to my hair
my skin all my clothes // too often the cause for the kids at
school // to smell me coming // squeeze faces into judgment
and looks of disgust // its flavor more important than my
chances at anyone ever // wanting to get close

Baby whimpers under Aunty's squeeze
and I almost don't notice
Aunty's fingers clenched
into the folds of my back
then the thick of my belly
then the roundness of my cheeks

I'm smiling at baby's soft skin
big brown eyes staring back
at me and I know for however
long she is here I will make sure
she is safe

**On the second day Aunty makes it known that nothing is
safe**
not the bathroom
not the kitchen
not the tv
not the closets
not the basement
not the garage
not the backyard
not any bedroom
not the living room
there would be no using up space
for dancing like some kind of
little monkey who forgot
she is a lady

she is the new woman of the house now
and things must change

And her first project is me:
How to Fix Your Fat American Niece

I made the terrible mistake
of letting Aunty braid my hair sunday night
before school the next morning

I specifically asked for small cornrows like
I'd seen Alicia Keys wearing on the red carpet

her soft and kinky curls cascading in perfect lines
flawless tight braids parted and woven back with beads on the
     ends

on the red carpet she had been the most glamorous tomboy
I had ever seen, donning tight jeans a leather jacket and
     sneakers

Aunty oblivious, did not catch the vision
her hands twisting and weaving my coarse strands into

thick plaits clad with heavy grease was not the plan, when she
     finished
I counted six horrendous things parted down the middle

the next day an eruption of laughter let loose in the middle of
     the hallway
all the black girls crashing into the lockers in disbelief

and pointing, me wrapping each finger tightly
around my books as I reached into my backpack for a place

to hide

Hide
/hīd/
verb
to put
or keep
out of sight
or
conceal from
the view or notice
of others

as in
when the girls
at school point
and laugh
in my direction
I wish that I
could hide

as in
I'm glad
Aunty isn't against
makeup cause
it's the only thing
helping me hide
the hair on my top lip

as in
when Aunty cooks
the stockfish
I always close
my bedroom door
stuff a towel under it   tight
making Dad and Aunty

EVERY BODY LOOKING

104

accuse me of shame
ask me

what it is I'm trying   to hide

I had learned I couldn't hide
far before the sixth grade
it had been five years
since I'd kept my first journal
five years
since that Chicago apartment
and saturdays with my father
taking sips of his coffee
while I slipped across
the floors in my
socks

Today Aunty acts like
it was just some book she found
tucked in the top sock drawer
while putting away laundry
that she didn't even do

she had no business in my things
but that didn't stop her from
snooping in places that did
not belong to her I guess

little girls aren't supposed to
keep secrets, even if
it was an adult who told you
this is just for you, that nobody

has the right to look inside
and judge your feelings here
you are supposed to trust
something that someone

can find and hold against you
like Aunty did to me that day
when I was trying again
because nothing is mine, not even

this

So you think your fahdah
is supposed to be by himself
you think he is all yours to keep
forever? she asks

you think all he's here to do
is raise you? *spend all his time*
on you?

never move on with his life?

I've never talked to Aunty
about Dad's loneliness
can not make out
what would make
her believe I'd think
something like this
about him
when I've eaten
popcorn I knew
I wouldn't like
laughed at all
his corny jokes
to make my father
happy
had always
discovered his smile
a big part of what
my life is for

But what I discover now
is that fire can live in your bones
that betrayal can
strike the match and light your
greatest fears ablaze

where I couldn't believe the words
I'd written for myself
about the women I didn't like
who weren't Mama

buying me things to be with my father
had been seen by someone else

I vowed to myself to never do this again

I'd thought hiding it underneath
my mattress would be enough
to keep someone's hands from
reaching deep inside

I thought the word PRIVATE
would be a warning to someone
who may not know if they should read

I thought the word PRIVATE
could still somehow mean
don't touch

I thought PRIVATE
was a place I could feel safe enough
to speak and not be made fun of

or spanked
or called names

somewhere I knew I would be believed

I look up at Aunty
my head hanging too heavy
with what I know I can't say

bouncing back and forth between
wanting to slap the smirk
off her face and wanting to
ease the burn behind my eyelids
wanting to cuss and stomp and
demand that she give me back
my privacy my space everything
she has taken by using my words
against me

she shifts her body in the chair
but keeps her eyes locked on
mine, her smirking turning to
full-blown smile then ugly laugh
knowing full and well she has
taken the thing she believes
no child should have and
there is nothing I can do
about it

Back upstairs and in my room-not-room
I slam the door closed
behind me with all
the force my arm
can give
bury my face
in a pillow
soak it
with hot tears
and muffled scream

An hour later I rise
from a heavy sleep, drenched
in the stink and wet of sweat
dressed in sad fatigue,
my room a tornado of everything that
once lived in the pink dresser
Dad bought me

the way my family sees me
I am still only in the second grade   with nothing
I can safely call mine

I count twenty
of the first pages
once written only
for my eyes
grab
scissors
cut
rip
go to the toilet

flush

In this house
I've learned that children
do not raise their voices to adults
do not accuse adults of being wrong
do not accuse adults of disrespect
according to tradition, all of that
is impossible

The sixth grade was already impossible
without Aunty's return to change everything / now I can't eat
without permission / I can't watch tv without permission /
it's now my job to clean the kitchen / as the oldest child / as
the first daughter / learning her duties as a future wife / and
mother / who was going to understand / that all I wanted to
learn / was how to make friends / at school

At school I was the funny black girl
my voice an instant punchline
my body an awkwardly shaped and useless pile of flesh
my hair styled too many years back
my clothes carrying the stench of stockfish and pepper soup

my father too proud to understand
being different meant being alone

Sometimes when I'm alone
I'm on a stage / there are lights / tons of lights coming from
every direction / there are people in seats before me / their
eyes glued to the jerk of my shoulders / the sway of my hips /
the rhythm of my feet moving too fast for them / too smooth
and I am perfect for the beat / my arms fling up and so does
my body / I leap like I know this / I move like I'm seen

COLLEGE

I leave the cafeteria unseen just in time
to witness Sophia
finally making her
way into the building
with all her potential boyfriends

heard her voice before
seeing her face
heard her heels before
seeing them descend

from the first floor
into the basement
where the cafeteria is
and realize that everyone

who's poppin gets there late

I technically can't be late to anything yet
cause class doesn't start
until next week so I figure
I can wander this building
where the smells of the cafeteria
rise above it

there are halls leading to offices
on the first floor and a ballroom
on the second where I hear
music blasting

for us new students on campus
every corner of this place
sounds like the parties
I've never been to

so I stay on the first floor
and dip into one of the halls
to look through everything
I can find posted

on the walls

On the walls of a college campus
you can find flyers to:
get your hair done *just as good as in a salon*
join weird clubs that are a *safe space*
try out for *a team that wins*
protest *this fascist administration*

audition for the dance program

apply
for a job

Dad said he would send me money
every month so I could focus on school
but I knew he'd use that to control me
parents paying for their kids to be in college
still try to tell you what to do from across the country

but Dad wasn't technically paying
a scholarship means being here is what
being smart earned me after all those nights senior year
spent doing homework while kids my age partied

I cringe remembering those nights
my head bent over math books under a small desk light
crunching imaginary numbers and symbols
now remembering I still have to buy those books here too

think back to parents weekend
upperclassmen upended over horror stories
where they'd spent hundreds
on textbooks for classes failed for being boring

I shake my head bringing myself
back into this hallway eyeing the flyer
for the job that had emails attached
at the bottom for everyone to pull

I pull one and feel the flyer
with the dancer on it burning a hole into my chest

I stare back
take one of those

too

EVERY BODY LOOKING

•

The dance department is too close
not to go look
I'm new here
so I have
every excuse
to walk down hallways
look into rooms
open doors
watch people
I don't know

I'm making sure I'm not seen here
walking
just past dark studios
quiet and empty
hardwood floors
glistening like
they were freshly polished
for chosen feet
I peak around
the corner
of a door cracked
exposing a soft ray
of sunlight
see her here
by herself

hair pulled back
in a headwrap
oversized t-shirt
catching the air
feet bare with
spread toes gripping
the ground
watch her
run back and forth
across this studio
rewinding the music
keeping the volume
low
but loud enough
for her to feel

find it strange seeing her
face all the mirrors

smiling playfully into them
as if telling herself
yes that's it
get it, girl

then stopping
when she stumbles
suddenly screaming
NO
DO IT AGAIN

In high school I had overheard the girls at church
talking about dance classes

I figured I would go   someday
if it's a class that would make me a student
if I'm a student they'll expect me to make mistakes

I'm always making mistakes
but maybe this is something I could try
I would hear them talk and talk

about who taught what
whose class was the hardest
how long they were training

would eyeball their beautiful bodies
their sculpted arms
firm thighs

told myself I wanted that
I wanted to *be* that
I wanted to make my body do that

too

I don't know what you're supposed to do
when you come across something you aren't
supposed to be watching
when all of a sudden you see something
that might be someone else's secret

like something tucked inside a pocket
something pressed underneath a bed
something within a locked notebook
something kept behind a cracked door

but there are mirrors everywhere
surrounding and following a body
a girl who isn't expecting
to be seen

I'm sure making a sound
I'm sure exposing yourself
isn't what you do

no

definitely not that

Dad always used to say that I don't know where my mouth is
so when I go to take that last big sip
from my water bottle, missing
my mouth
it was no surprise
to feel the cold splash
come down
my chin
come down
my neck
then soak
my chest

and though
it'd already happened
trying to stop it
I jump
knocking the door
I was hiding behind
further open
loudly
looking back up
to her stopped
standing still
staring back at me

We couldn't have been staring
at each other
for more than five seconds
five seconds
is all it really takes
to blow a first impression

to remember a face

I don't think I've ever turned
around so fast as I do today
not stopping when behind me
I think I hear the girl say something like
wait
or maybe she's telling me
that I shouldn't have been here
that this isn't my space

I don't wait to find out
or look back to see if she's
standing there
watching me run off
after she's caught me
studying her

like a creep

Too many things creep into my dreams
that night

the fact
that in the next bed
there is a girl I
I share a room with
sleeping

the fact
that she's probably already
got plans to bring one of those boys
she met

back here soon

the fact
that I ran away the first chance
I got to make a new friend
today

and stupidly
made my first gyno appointment ever
at the student health clinic
for tomorrow

I'd never done *it* before
but all the signs
in my new dorm

tell me everybody's been
doing something I haven't

figure that *it* is something
that might happen soon

figure I should go
to the school clinic anyway, ya know

before I even thought
about doing *it*, already

seeing these posters in the stairway
pamphlets on the way through campus

talking about knowing
your status, and

how we could catch
anything on contact, and

making sure
you're clean

now having to share showers
a nasty bathroom

and a whole floor with
girls I don't know

an old twin bed that on sight makes me itch
with all its . . . *history*

I make my appointment the first sign I see
cause for students it's free

and clean? I already feel
anything but

I heard
you're supposed to go
when you turn eighteen or
or when you've stopped being
a good girl

well I'm eighteen now and
I guess it's time
so I walk into that old
brick building that smelled of
latex and cough syrup
on the corner
of Shaw and Fourth street
so they could look at me

make sure everything's
all right
make sure
I'm normal
cause this is what I'm supposed
to be doing at eighteen

taking care of things
taking every step to be safe

9:00 AM is when they told me to be here
now checked in
sitting in a chair
waiting for someone

to call my name
ask me questions
about what I've done

just the way
Mama has always
accused me, they'll ask

who I've done it with
cause doctors get to ask
those kinds of things

so when they call me
I follow the nurse to the back
prepare for the routine

feeling like
a real college girl
who's doing it right

Fifteen minutes later the questions are over
and I'm on my back

here like I have to be
but suddenly my body is so dangerous
I can't control it

they've called back the nurse
to give me her hand
and she obeys

just beneath this gown

nothing but my naked body
spread for the woman with gloves

a light shining bright
enough to see the place
where I am both dead and alive

my heels rest
in the plastic cups along
each side of her

she tells me
we are going to do this
my body, having heard this demand before

begins to kick from its bottom
begins its convulsions
begins its ritual

where nothing can numb me
where I am possessed by my own fear

Before I can take this back
I see that I am already here
I am already naked
I have already said yes to
this thing women who've come
of age must do

before we can waste
any more time
she is already two gloved fingers inside me
probing for anything
abnormal

I have already tightened
my fist, purpling the nurse's fingers
a little girl who lives inside me
is demanding that this stops
feels knives clawing at her middle

is wondering if it will always
feel like the first time
someone touched me
inside

There are things they tell you get easier with time
that one day you'll grow up
and be able to take it all

they say this is what you have to do
to be an adult
this is what you have to do
to survive

you will not own your body
you will not own your things
you will not own your feelings

you belong to the world
to them
to Him

No one told me
that the room would be this small
that I would be this small
that the nurse would treat me small
would ask me questions
about the first time
and this would be my first time
so I would have nothing to say
and they would keep asking

they would laugh in my swelling face
they would ask me more questions
my pounding head would spin
I would wet the table beneath it
my knees would become a tremble

the nurses would look up
beyond my unyielding body

they would ask me
if somebody
had ever touched me
down there

Down there
is forbidden
is a safe with no key
is a hazard
is a pit bull's jaw snapped
is a venus flytrap
is a danger zone
is a dungeon
is a clenched fist
is a place you don't touch
is a place he touched anyway
is a place I could not talk about
is a private thing
is secret
is unknown
is reason my head
hung low, leaving
my eyes only
proud enough
to trace
my feet

FIRST GRADE

Ever since I could remember
Dad
had a problem with me
staying too long at Granny's house
said
a lot of people
go in and out of there
said
the people on the first floor
never saw what happened
upstairs
said
I don't feel good
about you staying overnight
but I would beg

and he would
say
okay

It was okay
to do a lot of secret things
in Granny's eight-bedroom house

this old three-story box of stuff
where Mama had most of her firsts

we would slide down the stairs
lying on our backs

we would hide in forts built
from pee-stained mattresses in the tv room

we would sneak and eat the penny candy
Granny sold to all the kids on the block

we would play every game
we could make up from morning

till it was dark

What was with adults
and upstairs
and behind closed doors
and with the lights turned off

they all seemed afraid
or oblivious
to the violently joyous

things young boys and girls
could do that mimicked
their mothers and fathers

the rhythmic squeak
of a bedspring
when all eyes in the house were shut

the front door cracking
to usher in
a stranger's sneakers from

the outside
when anything of the night
could be brought in like dust

But this dust was a boy
coming through the door   in the dead of night   just to lay
    down, he said

butbegan   topressahardthing   againstme   thedarkness

giving him   permission to touch   my everything   this time

a thing Daddy   said grown-ups should never touch   but what
    was my

cousin?   a grown-up?   a man.   and I?   a girl?   six?

a kid.   said this was   to be kept   under my bathing suit

under my panties   my cousin,   having different parents
    mustn't have

learned   the same thing

said

hushmoveyourhand
openyourlegs
doesthisfeelgood

I said
no.

After that night I don't like
any of my clothes

        all of them beginning

to fit too tight

        around my chest and thighs

my belly poking out

        a little at the bottom

my butt becoming

        big enough to see

big enough for boys

        to try and squeeze cheeks

slyly as they walk past

        another hush game

I suddenly hate

        these matching short sets

Daddy bought me

        in pink, purple, red

none of it screams

        loud enough

none of it screams

        hands off

this girl

        all of it making it

too easy to see

        what I got

underneath

Days later Daddy drops me off at Granny's again
and we are playing some type of game
my cousins do not explain, but begin to
play when all the grown-ups are out

to play this game all you need is your
body and questions like *what if* and
what would you do if I and *how come*

cousin asks me *what would you do if*
I squeezed your titties right now and
everyone laughs at this strange joke

I laugh not understanding the question
not understanding the test, I look him
in the eye, mean like Daddy taught me

and tell him   *I would slap you*

My daddy never said
it was good to fight
but if someone was
stupid enough to put
their finger in my mouth
they are looking
for me to bite

FIRST GRADE •

151

SECOND GRADE

Tonight Daddy and I enter
this strange building
we have never been to
where he holds my hand and
says nothing

I know this means
we're going somewhere
I would refuse to go
had I known before this minute

he tells me we are going
to the eighth floor and then
lets me press the number
eight

as if this will feel like
some kind of accomplishment
as if this will take my mind
from this dark unknown place

The eighth floor
is a place where we're welcomed only by the ding
of this slow and dim elevator that Daddy
still holds my hand strangely in

my hand becoming a damp home
of all of my questions

I know we're getting closer
to wherever we're going
after the eighth beep
and a quick bouncing jerk
where this lifting thing stops rising

right after the jerk the silver doors
that have been protecting
me and Daddy all this way split open
releasing us to what looks like
somebody's house

There are two couches
and a chair
black and
leather

a glass table
with all
kinds

of magazines, these
are something
to

do while we
wait for
whatever

is coming, I
tell Daddy
that

I'm scared
and that
I

want to go
home and
think to tell him

I take back
whatever
I said

the other day

Daddy gives my hands a quick
squeeze and says,
it's okay, Nwa m,
you can tell
Doctor Matthew
all about how
you're scared

you can tell the doctor
whatever you want

Before I can cry
and tell Daddy that
he should have told me
that we were going to the
doctor, that
he should have told me
we were coming *here*
where a *man* named Matthew
is going to get to ask me
all kinds of questions
about things
I don't know, that
he should have told me
so I could tell him
I don't want to go to
some *doctor* with a name
from the bible
on the eighth floor
of this building
that is too quiet
and too dark

before I can bury my face
into the side of Daddy's leg

and scream NO

the door flies open
and an old white man
in a suit, no
hair at the top
says *WELCOME!*
with a strange smile

The way Doctor Matthew smiles
is like he knows something I don't
so I already know I don't like him

what kind of *doctor* is this who has us
come see him at night in this strange room

with a table, that has chairs around it
like my daddy's office and where are

all the nurses and the ladies at the front
desk to take our names and the ladies

who come to take my height, my weight
and my blood?

There is nothing in this room
but this table
and these chairs
and that lamp
some toys
and us

I go to the toys while
Doctor Matthew looks
at both me and Daddy
like he doesn't know
how much

my daddy has told me
if anything
comes to sit with me
on the floor
asks
so how are you feeling
today, little girl?

and I just roll the yellow truck
with its red wheels across
the carpet, back and forth
look back
wonder
if this is a stranger
that I can talk to
wonder
how long this *doctor*
has known my daddy
wonder
if I should
tell the truth

I had dropped Daddy's hand
seeing
the toys thinking
it was safe to let go
and I look to my left
where he sits above and next
to me like stone and question mark
at the same time. his hand rubbing

across the folds at the top of his rippled face
as if he is pushing aside waves crashing against
his fingers, the way he does when he's both tired and
without answers. but says *go on. it's okay. tell the doctor*
what you told me

And I wonder if I can say no
today I am meeting Doctor Matthew
cause I told Daddy that I miss Mommy
cause I cry in my sleep and it's the only thing that comes out

the only thing that makes sense

I try to make sense
of all the things my mind

tells me to say to this doctor

my mind wandering up
to the bare space of his

pale scalp and him leaning
in for my next breath

his reeking of
cigarettes and coffee

and I give him what he wants,
I want my mommy, I say

he replies,
*I know. and how does that
make you feel?*

Who is this Doctor Matthew
and what are these toys here for
if he won't just let me play

I want to tell him that I like
that this small toy truck is yellow

and how yellow is my favorite color
how when I look at it, I feel like summer

and how I like that
the wheels are bright red

just like Mommy's
lipstick

Little girl how does that make you feel
he asks again
and behind him I see
the toy with all the beads
and it looks kind of like a maze
but not really cause I know where
the beads have to go to get to the end

but maybe it is a maze cause the beads
can't ever get out

Your daddy told me
you've been sad
what do you like
to do when you feel sad

I want to tell him
that I like to play
and that I can't
get to the other toys
when he is sitting
in front of me asking

questions

my left hand squeezes
the roof of the yellow truck
pushes it hard and lets it fly
crashing hard into the wall past
Doctor Matthew's leg

my right hand shoves
the beads I was gliding
to the other side of the maze
and the loud smack
makes me laugh from my belly

Daddy's face twists curiously hearing it

I want to keep laughing
like this, close my eyes
and picture someone else
coming to play with me
picture Doctor Matthew
not being so close

But instead my chest begins
to burn and then my arms and then neck and then my face
becomes so hot I don't know what's boiling inside it / I look
to Daddy to see if he heard this stupid question / also to
question how this doctor *knows* about Mommy / and then back
at *Doctor* Matthew / and then back to my hands / I wonder to
myself why I'm here and why we needed this old white man
who is too fat / to ask me a question that Daddy could have
asked / on one of our saturdays together / where I would slide
along the freshly mopped hardwood floors / in between sips of
his coffee / in between the small tasks I was given around the
house / Daddy could have asked this / and then we wouldn't
be here / me, scared and searching for new words for this same
feeling / this burning behind my eyes / and I reply, *I told you, I
miss her* and think / doesn't that say how I'm feeling, enough?

This becomes a back-and-forth
that lasts many more minutes, where
this doctor is taking notes and staring
too long and too deeply into the many
movements of my face as I spit answers
to questions coming from a stranger
I just met today

what I get at the end of all of this
is thick with lined paper, one spiraled
silver coil that begins at the top and ends
at the bottom, its cover a strange shade
of green mixed with blue and all mine to
scribble and draw inside

Daddy and the stupid doctor
stand to shake each other's hands
this is how I know it is time to leave
but am glad I am leaving with this
small gift I hold it tightly to my chest
and smile, avoiding the doctor's eyes

I don't hold my daddy's hand
on our way back to the two silver
doors that will take us back down
to the street I do not hold his hand
again for a while

COLLEGE

Standing in the doorway back in my dorm room
wet-faced
when my phone rings
Dad somehow calls me now
to see how school is going
to see how I'm coping
I can't tell him
how I couldn't do this
how I couldn't do this one thing
that all women
are supposed to be able to do
I can't tell him
about the looks on their faces
the chuckles
the scoffs
I can't tell him
they were looking at me
like a little girl
I can't tell him
that I don't know
why I was so scared
instead I tell him
through sniffles
being away from home
is hard
so many tests
and new people here
and he tells me
god is with me
that I'll be fine
if I just
stay in my books
tells me
that he knows
because he prays

We always say amen at the end of prayer
when amen spread out
into two words
spells   *a-men*

which doesn't even
make sense
when there is only either

a man
or many men
either way

was taught early
one man or many men
only want one thing

and it starts
when they're still
just boys

To the boys
next to others
like my roommate
I was still just a girl anyway
soft and quiet and new
probably figure I'd be
too ashamed
to tell secrets
probably think
this one would be easy

a glass-eyed doll
grateful for a look
a word
a hand
a smile
my way

Getting a job was one step on my way
to some kind of freedom
had one in high school and
had to get another if I was going
to abandon Dad's plan for my life
but getting one

with the school's basketball team
must be the worst job for women
looking to be taken seriously
given I'm the only girl
dumb enough to apply

just weeks
after calling a number I found
on a random flyer
just a floor above
the cafeteria

I get it
and start the same day

My first day
is sweat slick
with the hot funk of
season's first practice

towels flung
without looking
hampers Coach says to keep empty

do the laundry
get the water ready
never be late
do what he says
keep my mouth shut
if I want this job
to last

The first guy
I let take my mouth in his
would lead me up to the faculty lounge
in Robeson Hall where the security
guards would never check

the hallways lit

at all hours
with the lounge
a perfect opportunity
to hide

Derek

ugly and short
but nice to me, sometimes
told me *you got a smart mouf, you know dat?*

didn't care what came from it
as long as it made him feel good

I just liked
how he rested his hand
on the small of my back
and smirked warmly
when I would speak

me

he chose *me*
that had to mean something

right?

The moments would seem so right
just because
they were happening to me

the girl
Dad once said the boys
wouldn't want yet

the girl
Dad once said was silly
for crying
over the boys

the girl
Dad didn't prepare
for the ugly ones
the ones

so ugly
I didn't see
coming

I didn't see him coming
what?

       Derek. he likes you.

no he doesn't. he's just nice. he's not lookin at me like that.

       trust me. most of the guys on the team think you're cute.
       you want me to confirm it?

no they don't (WHAT!)

       whatever.

they don't. you're just fucking [must-sound-experienced] *with me*
    (REALLY?!)

       okaay.

       Derek's Facebook profile says single
       that dumb look permanently stitched
       across his face might actually be
       a wink
       and a smile

His stupid smile
is probably
what convinced me to go
with him and his stupid friends
to a movie

alongside the other girl
that he stupidly invited

he said that she's just his friend
that she didn't have the money
to pay for her own movie
that I could have at least paid

for my own
snack

we sat on each side
of him and his popcorn
his lips parting
to show teeth and drop stray kernels

every five minutes
me only in control
of the mess on this side

And I guess it wasn't that bad to not be in control
anyway right
it is the boy
who asks
the girl out
it is the boy
who pays
it is the boy
who makes
the first move
never mind if
the girl isn't
liking the
moves
he makes

But to be chosen by someone
was all the right
I needed for now

his eyes lasering my lips
him wanting me around

it really didn't matter
that I wasn't the only one

that she was in the dorm
across the street from mine

that we had never talked about this
that I didn't know how this even went

that the tears came with the truth
that all I wanted was to be the only

that all I needed was to be claimed

Dad claimed to know
all about how boys
were supposed to treat me

if he doesn't treat you better
than I treat you
he isn't good enough

but almost always
kept good enough to himself
kept his little girl close
kept his little girl blind
kept his little girl

wanting to know what *better* was

I didn't know I could find better
than Derek

all I knew was that he liked me
and that was reason enough
to hold on
to look the other way
when he went to go see her
when he brought me things
that weren't mine
when all we did was lay around
when laying around became
the only thing I knew
when the only thing I knew was
please

To please a boy
answer the phone
when he calls
respond
when he sends a message
be nice
when he is mean
be available
when he has time
be available
when she rejects him
be available
when he is bored
be ready
to be drafted
when she no longer
wants him
even if you
are just something
to do

He says
he likes me cause every time
he wants to chill, I'm free

and I was thinking
how each time he's free

I'm really not, and trapped
by the dank of a boy's dorm room

wishing his skin and lips
were actually soft

mad at this sad option
that looked nothing like what I want

him, what I might be able to have
him, a chance I should be grateful for

him tossing me a bone I reach for
cause it's the only kind

I believe I can reach

Reach
/rēCH/
verb
to stretch out
an arm
in a specified
direction
in order
to touch or grasp
something

---

as in
when I'm bored
in Derek's bed
sometimes
I reach for my phone
to watch
dance videos
on YouTube

as in
accounting class keeps
feeling like gym
cause every time I reach
for the textbook
I suddenly want
to sleep

as in
whenever Derek
needs something
to do
he calls me
but never

can be reached
when I need someone
too

as in
when I saw that girl
dancing by herself
in the studio that day
I wanted to know
if being confident
enough to do that
is something
I could ever
reach

A chance is all I've ever wanted
it was all I needed
to prove that I wasn't as lame
as everyone thought I was

college was
like everything else for me
a bunch of firsts

a first time
away from home
a first time
in a new bed
a first time
in new hands
a first time
to make a choice

on a new campus
where every day is a fashion show
and everyone
is also the smart black kid
in the class
trying to keep up
never works

so I just
tried to keep myself

The days I tried
to look like I knew
how to be here I failed

college at an HBCU was still more groups
and more cliques than high school

either more ways to fit in
or be left standing out

student government
sororities

marching band
athletes and

apparently girls
with head-wrapped afros

who dance by themselves
wearing oversized t-shirts

in empty studios
had a place around here too

I didn't know what boys wanted
but I liked to wear t-shirts
and cargo shorts to class

the occasional joke
about being
on the other team was silly
anyway

I didn't know there were other teams
wondering how one gets on the other team
without knowing how to play

what's wrong with a girl
wanting to be comfortable

what's wrong with keeping
what I had to myself

aren't us girls
all on the same team?

but it seemed like everyone
knew how to play this game

everyone but me

I already knew I was nothing like
the other girls
walking around like
they could fit their
mama's clothes

my hips didn't sway like that
my breasts were nearly nonexistent
is this what the boys want?
their mamas?

FIRST GRADE

Daddy never lied about Mommy

where is she?
why doesn't she live here?
who is that man?
who is the man that came
to pick me up?
why is that his name?
does Mommy like him better than you?
better than me?
does Mommy love that man?
is that man a stranger?
if he is a stranger, should I go with him?
why does Mommy yell?
why does she yell like that?
does Mommy love me?
then why can't I be with her?
where
is
she?

She doesn't live far from us
you can call her
if you want
I will dial her phone number
for you
better yet
use
your new journal
remember
the therapist said
you can draw pictures
when you feel sad
pictures
when you miss her
pictures
for what you feel
inside
pictures
when you don't have
the words
pictures
when she doesn't answer

Things I could do at Mommy's house

1. Put as much sugar in my bowl of Cheerios as I wanted.
2. Fall asleep in front of the tv. I didn't have a bed there anyway.
3. Sleep on the couch. I didn't have a room there anyway.
4. Shave my legs like the big girls. One day.
5. Watch rated R movies. Especially the ones Daddy had already said no to.

Because I'm her goddamn daughter too.

The truth was that sometimes
she would not answer
when I said it *too much*

four very bad words
I love you, Mommy

said, I told her this
too much

asked what I needed
to say those words so much for

told me, *okay*
that's enough

Three days visiting became enough
and
when we rose
on the third day
the first thing
she would ask is
when I would like
to go back
to Daddy's house
because this was home *too*
today
tomorrow
or the next day
in my heart
I would want to say
today
but knew
the day after tomorrow
was better to say
to Mommy
saying today
was a bad idea
was a joke
was an insult
was what ungrateful little girls say
to their mommies
who they should miss
would hurt her feelings
too much
and everything was bad
when Mommy hurt

Mommy could not put her hands where she hurt
she hurt where I could not see
waking in the night's middle
on my weekend visits
would mean waking
to her deep sobs
about something I never would know
when I never knew mothers could
cry like their children
her sadness
hung stale
like the aroma of bacon smoke
and chicken grease
long after the house had been fed
and Mommy was too tired and scarred
to feed
herself

Going back to Daddy's house
was always a long drive
in silence
filled with shame and grief
for not wanting to stay with my mother

who left an aftertaste
bitter of another person leaving

abandoning her after she
had done nothing
but open
her arms

COLLEGE

It's a month into my first semester
and I've been here
long enough to know
it's time to execute
my plan somehow

on tuesdays and thursdays
they make us
wear suits to class
like robots

an outdated conformist ritual
of pretend professionalism
forced on us black kids
if we want success

thirsty for As
hungry for nods
from our professors
like a good call home

I'm not homesick
or some other word
for sad being miles from
my family like everyone else

seems to be
but something's definitely
got me ready
to get out

Class gets out early today
I rush for the door
to avoid Derek

we've got classes together
and having to see him
later at practice

is more than
enough

having learned
that nothing

is more awkward
than seeing a boy
you don't really like

and who's kinda
seen you naked
in the daylight

except running into a girl
you once ran from
but want to know

Where you runnin to
this time
Happy Feet?

she's already given me
a corny nickname
but I'm the one who's embarrassed
and even though it's been a month
recognize her immediately
as I stop
feeling caught
she's shorter than I remember
my eyes already searching her
before I can pretend
I'm not
suddenly realizing
she's asked me a question
still hoping Derek
is somewhere walking
the other way

I'd be ready to turn the other way again
but she's smiling
still staring into my face
her whole stance a question
waiting for me to stop being dumb
and answer

I tell her
my dorm

try to be smooth
and ask
and you?

well I'm not running
anywhere like you
just coming from the studio

you remember the one
right?

Before I can squeeze out a full apology
for spying on her
she stops me with her laughter
tells me to chill
that it's okay
tells me it's been
a long time
since she's had
an audience

but how
I ask

don't they make you
dance in front of everyone
all the time
in class?

she laughs at me
again
tells me
she doesn't even
go to school here

Name: Kendra
AGE: *19*
FROM: *DC, born & raised*
JOB: *studio assistant, over at the one in NE*
DREAM: *To dance*
HOW: *Whenever, wherever I can learn*

for free
cause I don't need
to pay nobody all that money
to do what's already
in my heart

I guess it's my heart
that's racing now
walking through campus
almost forgetting that
I was trying not to be seen
just minutes before

and here is this stranger
who sneaks onto campus
maybe the first who is
seeing me   talking to me
who maybe wants to be my friend

SECOND GRADE

Back in the second grade I knew better
than to be touching Sarah
right there in the classroom
under the desk
while the teacher
had her back to us

it was sort of a game
we played
who could tickle
the other until she
laughed but

neither of us
laughed we just
touched and asked
for the hall pass
just minutes
after the other
to continue the
the secret game
we had no name for

To give this game a name
                                    would be to say
                                    that we were playing at all

but we were not

this was not   happening

it did not   feel good

we didn't   meet in the second stall
                                    in silence
                                    with the clasps
                                    of our ashtray jeans
                                    undone
                                    and far below our knees

we were not   in there together

my fingers didn't   slide from just below
                                    her navel

                                    nor glide beneath her underwear

we weren't   gone
                                    for that long
                                    with the hall pass

On our way back we would pass
two water fountains
we needed stools to reach
four closed classroom doors
with barking teachers on the other side

sometimes
one bad child who was sent
to take a break for talking too much

Sarah's open hand
would become hers and mine
two moist bunches
of stubby fingers
holding each other
briefly

her cheeks flush
of blotchy maroon and smile
mine of damp brown and giggle

all of this disappeared
when time
delivered us back
to class

The class would sometimes
be
lined
up
at
the
door
when
we
made
it
back
we
had
to
pass
by
every
questioning
eye
who
wanted
to
know
where
we
had
been
when
we
had
asked
to
go

at
different
times
and
now
the
class
would be punished together when we arrived to gym   late

In the late months of spring
parent teacher conferences
would come back around
Daddy would show up
to the place of my secret adventures

I would hold my breath
and the teacher would talk
Daddy would look down at me
they would laugh about
how my mouth was always running

smile about my grades
and Daddy's accent
later Daddy would ask questions
then would believe my answers

I would just be happy
that I
survived

Survival in my neighborhood
didn't seem as tough
as they said it would be
for black kids living in chicago
but this was the north side

two blocks from school was where
Daddy and I slid across hardwood floors
on saturday mornings and I would beg
for coffee while we cleaned the apartment
top to bottom and the answer was always
yes

Our apartment
was a block each way
from a corner store
some saturday afternoons
I would walk
two houses down
and Stacie and Kate
would find us something
to do

candy

we could go get candy
without money
without parents
there are ways
to get it on our own
Stacie would say
we do this all the time
Stacie would say

                    but how

my mouth had always been
the problem
if I would have just
slid the packs
into my pocket
without whispering
down the aisle
the lady at the front
would have never known

Daddy had never known
that I was taking things
I was being taught how
to take things we had the money for

on saturday
mornings I got to pick out
almost
whatever I wanted
from the same store
paid for
with Daddy's dollar bills

each time I would choose
to fill my belly with
clear fizzy liquids
to chew till my jaws grew sore
the magical magenta jugs
that were packed with
sweet dust that
turned to bubble gum
and
salty chips crisp with
orange cheddar and
speckled ranch

but the day
my favorite things
did not slide easily
into the back pocket
of my jeans
a day Daddy had allowed me
to go play with those Oyibo (*white*) girls
down the street, whose daddy called me a bad name

that my daddy would not repeat and I didn't understand
the cashier's hand stopping my wrist
mid disappearing act
the jig
way more than up
I knew I would have
to tell
one of my first lies

COLLEGE

Laying on my back in Derek's room
seems to be the natural order of things

he doesn't talk much
and when he opens his mouth
mocking questions always come out
like

why does everything have to be about god
and
but I didn't ask you about Jesus
and
you a slick one huh?
and
that mouth of yours gon get you in trouble, girl

I sometimes ask what about
my mouth was trouble
why he can't be the someone
who has time for all my questions
my body awkwardly tucked in the nook
between his chest and arm

find his answers make me tired
left feeling alone even under covers this close
knowing he likes me better laid silently
under him like this

so I figure since I'm here
and in his bed
the best thing to do with my mouth
is kiss
and kiss
and kiss

Kissing is the best thing
until it's time to do more
and when you're kissing
you can close your eyes
and pretend this mouth you're kissing
belongs to the most beautiful person
in the world
that the rest of his body
is just as soft as his lips
come close to being
and that this all
actually means something
like love
like warmth
and you'll grow into it
this thing
will be
real

I had never been in a real relationship
before Derek
the day I confirmed
I was good enough
to kiss
or hold hands
or one day lay
in his bed
was the same day
I thought we were
automatically   together

Be ye not
unequally yoked
with unbelievers

for what fellowship hath
righteousness with unrighteousness

and what communion hath
light with darkness

Paul's letter
to Corinthians

calls Derek and me
out by our names

let a woman learn
quietly with all submissiveness

I do not permit a woman to teach
or to exercise authority over a man

rather, she is
to remain quiet

the second chapter
of First Timothy

making man and god
sound the same

the heart is deceitful
above all things

and desperately sick;
who can understand it?

the seventeenth chapter
of Jeremiah

a mockery of me back
in a boy's bed lost

I have never really seen my parents together
except for the day of my
high school graduation

the idea of my father and mother
ever sharing

a house
a life

as one
is as strange

as a bat sighting
in downtown Peoria, Illinois

the place of my earliest
childhood memory and

the last time
my parents lived in the same city

after deciding
when I was one

that love
isn't forever

SECOND GRADE

Daddy has a new girlfriend
and when we pull up to our apartment
she floats from my daddy's car
like she's been here before

as if her own home
in Nigeria was
just around the corner

from our street on the north side
of Chicago where we've lived
for a year now

she doesn't
speak much to me
but is more than familiar

with him

When fathers get new girlfriends
there are suddenly two girls in the house
everyone walking on eggshells

cause girlfriends are new and I am not
but somehow they get to sleep with Daddy

talk to Daddy, late into the night
when I am supposed to be in bed

their voices moving in laughter or
screaming, privilege to use

mature tone but not wake
me from my sleep

Suddenly it seems like

I am always here at the wrong time

flashes of pale bare flesh flicker in sight

when Daddy's bedroom door is cracked

her skin the soggy color of Cheerios

made me wonder how much

of its bareness she let him touch

a woman Daddy treats like a mommy

fixing her lipstick in the bathroom mirror

being seen at our dinner table

watching things on our tv

sharing in our nightly prayers

saying no in response to Daddy's

squeeze to join in and

lead them

too

She has now been here for a week
and this night I cannot sleep
hearing something like a tussle
a fight, words flinging midair
like knives, Daddy's girlfriend
raising her voice high

hearing names
hearing words
hearing things
we do not say
in this house

I emerge from my room, barebacked
to the dark of our dim living room
the two of them facing
each other like opponents
in a dogfight

my father hastily requests
that I go back to sleep
and I just want her to
know that I can
hear

***You see that**
you woke my child
with your mouth

my child doesn't know
this kind of disrespect

my child doesn't even know
who you are

and she definitely doesn't
know anything about

a woman raising her voice
to a man

I have seen my mother
raise her voice to several men
called them names I cannot repeat
names you should never call someone
you love

sometimes someone you love was me
when I wasn't being called
ungrateful and/or a wench
I was a bitch

a little girl who dressed herself like
some little boy scraping and bloodying
her knees in the street
this is when I learn

a woman who fears no man, fears
nothing—not even the marking she
will leave on her child—not even the
one on me

Adults never think
that we are listening
that us kids can hear
the things they say to
each other about us
the things they say
to us about each other
they must think we
see everything as
play

The next morning
I lay across from
the frame resting on the shelf
just as I always do
this frame holding
the only photo I own
of my mother
its colorful lines
designed like
crayon scratch
next to each other
shaping to form
the words
I LOVE MY MOMMY

I remove
the picture it holds

replace it
with the one
Daddy has gifted me
of this new woman

I will tell him
there is no reason
I will tell him
it is just a frame

any good picture
can be placed
inside it

We meet in the bathroom
when I have come to do my business
she has come to apply another shade
I slowly eyeball her plump shape while
she tells me to carry on cause I've said
this is my private time, tells me I have
nothing she hasn't seen before, that
the two of us have the same things, I
should *stop being so foolish and just pee,* I see her
lean into the glass, press her lips together
and out as if to kiss the woman in her
reflection, draws the creamy stick of red
across the length of her mouth, back and forth
does this until it is as if she has sucked
the last of my favorite Popsicles, as if
all that is good and perfect is for her
to devour, puts the cap back on to
the same shade of lipstick my mother
wears and chuckles to herself, flings the
door open and leaves with it left wide
the doorway breeze throwing a cold slap
to my halfway naked body
before I even get the chance
to flush

And I don't even get a chance
to wipe before I am thinking about me
having nothing she hasn't seen before

look down and touch the two bumps
on my chest, look to see what is tucked

between my knees

the cold gust from the hallway coming
through the door making my skin a land

of small hills I shiver, flush, wash
my hands, wonder what else she sees

On the drive back to the airport
no one is speaking
I hear nothing but
the water coming heavily
from the sky
against the windshield

sliding down into
the street
wipers
creating rhythm
and dance
at the same time
and seeming
to be the only things
happy
inside this car
besides me
seeming
to be waving
goodbye
to this woman
who raised her voice
to Daddy
for the last time

When we get back home under my mattress
I go back to my notebook / its silver coils now smashed almost flat / under my body every night / the edges of the cover now beginning to look tired of me / and my stupid shapes and lines it's been holding / from Daddy / from this new woman / from Mommy / from me / I lift the cover of this stupid thing to look inside the pages / like it is a book / someone else has written / like it is a story about a girl / far away from me / I see scribbles and a few words with pictures / looking a lot like my insides / looking a lot like my brain / everything inside a mess with no meaning / everything a secret mess / like me

I know the doctor and Daddy
want me
to draw something   anything
about missing
my mother

but all
I can
think about
is that

night, flashes
of memory
that don't
make any

sense, that
with each
day, my
shame tucks
it away
even more

COLLEGE

I just love the way I feel
when I'm doin it, you know
like can't nobody tell me
I'm wrong or that what I feel
ain't the truth

sure some of these girls is
skinnier and got
better posture
than me

prancin up and down
these studios, legs flyin
all high up in the air
with their asses tucked in

like they better than us
cause they been trainin
for years, she says
leaning back

on her elbows across my bed
like it's hers and like she's
been here
a thousand times before

but you know what?
they can't teach these
barbies on pointe
how to dance from the CHEST

ain't no book for that shit
she says releasing
her elbows out, hands stacked under her head
her back all the way down closing her eyes

So why do you think
they're paying
all this money
to be here, then

if you don't
really need
to be classically

trained
to dance
I question

Because they're dumb
she replies, without opening her eyes
how you think those little African kids
on Youtube and Instagram learned
to move like that?

never seen a ballet class
in they whole life
but they be GETTIN IT
out here killin the game

tell me
THAT
ain't real technique

people out here payin
thousands of dollars when all
they ever need is their feet and a beat

You don't pay
to learn to dance?
I ask Kendra

well yeah,
but not no overpriced tuition

where they make me
read shit I don't wanna learn

she says eyeballing
my accounting 101 textbook

now beginning to collect dust

I want to learn
from who I want

and I do it
on my own terms

besides, they still out here
acting like ballet

is the holy grail of dance

like . . . ain't this a black school?

Kendra had a point
that week she'd already
shown me like fifty videos
of these dancers
all over Instagram
with millions of likes
and they were African just like me . . . sort of

moving to drums or songs
that sounded like the music
my dad and his friends played
at Nigerian parties or what
I used to hear in class
without a pointed toe
in sight

but I know
somebody had to have
taught them

I know you don't just
wake up knowing how
to move like that

I mean come on, now
look at the Tofo Tofo Dance Group for example
THE Beyoncé was callin THEM
for her "Run the World" video—
not the other way around

fuck technique
she says mockingly with air quotes
I'm just tryna be smooth with it
like them and all my ancestors

so smooth can't nobody
tell me I ain't
clean

All right, all right
you got it
I say, ending
today's debate
having already
learned in just
four days
that there's
no argument
Kendra doesn't win

but I kinda liked
losing, given
I always learn something new
and she's the first person
on campus to care
enough about what I
had to say
to really fight it

She's now got her feet on my bed
thumbing through
my textbooks stacked
on the side

but I don't fight it

I think she's my friend already
even though there's still
room for things to happen

still room for me to mess things up

SIXTH GRADE

Today I don't care
that everyone is staring
as I make my way to the back
of the classroom where the only seat
left open waits for me

the look my teacher throws my way
the quiet that takes over class when I arrive
the curious looks from my darkened upper lip
to my chubby waist
to my boyish clothing
can't bring me down from
the high I feel
knowing

after school I'm leaving my dad
to spend the weekend with my mama

Pulling up to my mama's driveway
I don't know which mother I'll get this time
but I'm happy

here I'm far from rules
Mama says I can do whatever I want

as long as I don't
start some shit

as long as I leave her
alone

But Mama and I are not alone
after Dad drives away
another car pulls up and Mama says

put on your shoes
we goin out to eat tonight

my man is paying
says

ooh! and we can stop after and get a movie
you can pick whichever you want

hurry up
we can't leave Jay waiting

I almost forgot
about Jay even though
Mama always had a man
and she had told me
she found a good one
over the phone

the scents of cigarettes, beer
and cheap cologne attack
my nostrils just after I close
his Cadillac's back door
how you doin, girl

he says

yo daddy let you out the house
to stay wit us, huh

I know the smell
creeping between Jay's
words and strange chuckle
cause Mama wears that scent too

they both seem to be in the perfect mood
and I'm hungry

Jay wasn't really waiting for me to answer
and we begin to pull off, his
right hand clutching
Mama's thigh

Mama's thigh moves
side to side
the way it does when she is giddy
or telling a story
or drunk

I think this is one of those times
when she is all three

And Jay tightens his squeeze
whenever we turn a corner
or whenever they laugh

They seem to be laughing
through our whole ride to the restaurant
and my stomach does flips as Jay pulls
the car into park

I don't know if this is hunger or fear

But I choose hunger and decide
to be happy that this meal will be
free

and Mama seems happy
so I just go along

And I go along with it
when Mama tells me that today
I am ten even though we know I am twelve

if anyone asks, you are ten
you hear me? we know
you're miss perfect

but just say you're miss perfect ten
today she says, mocking me

I nod and say
okay

When we've been seated
a menu for kids has been placed
in front of me that reads

Bite-sized Prices for 10 and Under
and I understand

I understand
what kind of night this will be
what kind of night Mama and I
will have sort of together
when she is staring
into Jay's eyes
mumbling things
I am not supposed to hear

what kind of night this will be
is what I know when the food
comes with a pitcher of beer
with glasses for each

so I pat my growling belly
try and trace the lines of
my cartoon place mat
that is for kids two years
or more below my age

and eat in silence

I don't notice the silence
is only in my head until
Mama's cackle jerks me
from my place mat trance

I had been watching
the lines curve and
loop and dance

around the page
with trivia questions
and matching numbers

to questions like
how many feet in a mile
how many marbles in this jar

could you escape this maze?

No one can really escape
Mama's laugh
usually set off like gunfire
at something only
she found funny

this time it was a joke
about how strict my daddy is
this time it was a joke
about my *proper* speech

I loved Mama's laugh
the way it would erupt
from her belly unexpected
and outrageous

I loved Mama's laugh
the way it didn't care
who was around
or who agreed

Mama's laugh
meant joy
meant she
was at peace

Before a storm there is always peace
and my belly is full
walking back to the car
with Jay and Mama hand-in-hand
clouds above us a weird gray under a blue-black sky

a light drizzle begins
to come down just before
we are in our seats, belted
and ready to head to Redbox to grab a movie

Mama alerts me
that Jay will be picking the movie
we will be staying in the car out of the rain
but, Mom, you said—

YOU JUST THINK YOU DESERVE
                    EVERYTHING

Jay is now back out
of the car
and Mama is screaming

WHY YOU ALWAYS GOTTA
ASK STUPID-ASS QUESTIONS

LIKE WE
AIN'T JUST PAY FOR EVERYTHING

LIKE WE
DIDN'T JUST FEED YOU

YOU THINK
YOU CAN "BUT MOM" ME?

I know better
than to answer any
of these questions

instead I stare
out my window

trying to count the stray
raindrops that fall

and are swirling down
the window and wonder

how they just form
patterns of water like that

how they never seem
out of place

how they just
know where to go?

COLLEGE

So do you wanna go or what?
at some point
in all this talk about
people paying to
go to school
to dance
it slipped
my mind that
Kendra had
asked me if
I wanted to
go to some
party

it had been
easy to change
the subject since
there was never
a time she couldn't
go off about dance
but the truth was
I was hoping
she forgot too

if I don't drink
and don't really
know anybody

if I don't drink
and some boy tries
to grind up from behind

what then
am I supposed to do?

Oh-uhh-yeah
I mean
I don't really uh
think I can go
cause you know
I got practice
I mean
I don't have practice
but the team does
you know I uh
gotta be there
with the team
Coach says
I always gotta
be there
uh you know
to do my job
you know
plus I gotta like
study
how that goes
I say shuffling clothes
aimlessly around the room

The party starts at eleven
so you know uh
you can like I mean
get your shit together
after work and uh
still go you know
if uh you're not
too uh tired
to kick it with me
she mocks

besides, do you SEE this dust?
she says dragging a finger
dramatically across
the accounting 101 cover
ain't nobody studying
up in here

somehow seeing
through my attempt
to get out of
dragging myself
through my first
awkward college party

She's stopped thumbing
through my bookshelf
now sitting straight up
watching me
looking *through* me

it's not you
that I don't
wanna hang out with
it's just that I—

she interrupts
my half-formed excuse
raising a stiff palm
toward me:
whoever it is
fuck em

we're going

TWELFTH GRADE

I've named her Magic
and every time I've drawn her
her toes point so tough
her whole leg glowed strong
with muscle and grace
just like my dance teacher
taught me

> Dad doesn't know it yet
> but I can *dance*

she's more than just
a pointed toe now
her sculpted body sprawls out
on the page like a giant X

her hands reach toward
the top corners
as if reaching out
to grab the sky

I named her Magic cause
she can do anything
jump, turn, move to
any music life plays

I played around a lot
in art class until today
when I bring in Magic
for Ms. Lesley to see

she says for the last
semester of our high school
careers we will study superheroes

I wait until the end of class
to share every piece
I've drawn Magic in

tell her these are nothing
tell her it's just something
I do when I feel sad

she glides her hand across
each as if she is just searching
for the truth

The truth is
I don't know why I keep drawing this body
that no one thinks of when looking at me
or why today I decide someone else should
see this character I want to be, this woman
I've seen leaping through all my dreams

And in my dreams of course
Magic is always dancing
in each scene
there is always an audience
waiting for the next thing

crowds part to see her stomp
and dip low
arch her back
and move

while the cuts in her muscles
gleam under a bright sun
or lights that shine
just as bright

She asks me why I brought her here
repeats *you have the next five months to study superheroes*
look at them, the way their bodies are drawn we see what they can
   do
I have never heard of this one before, who is she
superheroes use x-ray vision
superheroes have wings
superheroes move buildings
superheroes do unbelievable things
superheroes save

who will Magic save?

I know
she works hard
not to look at me
like I'm crazy
a seventeen-year-old girl
who's been drawing
a superhero
who doesn't have
someone
to save

but

Ms. Lesley just smiles
looks back and forth
between the sketches
of Magic and me

and says: *that's funny. Magic kind*
of looks like you

(really?)

What you may not know is this:
After the day Dad found me on the floor of my bedroom I
never shared my drawings again until today but there are
hundreds of her tucked in every corner of my things. Magic in
my backpack. Magic in my closet. Magic in my desk. Magic
under my bed. I didn't know how to draw faces so I studied
mine. I didn't know how to draw legs so I studied mine. I
didn't know how to draw arms so I studied mine. But I had
never worked out a day in my life so I had to upgrade her.
Started taking notes from anime even though sometimes Dad
looked at me strange cause the girls looked too much like
women and were *too sexy*. But they were magical cause their
bodies could fight and would win. That's how Magic got her
name.

COLLEGE

They call me by every name
but the one my mama and dad
gave me when I was born

running up and down the court
catering to musty butts and sweaty balls

you'd swear my real name was Shorty
New-New, or the African Chick if you took the team   seriously

but the only reason why I do is cause
the coach makes sure I get paid

and on some days basketball practice
was the only time I felt   like a woman

You'd swear they'd never
seen a woman
the way these idiots act
every time I step
into the gym
each monday
wednesday
and friday
for practice
wearing
the same thing
I had on
last time

whistles
stares
comments
an ongoing game
between them
to see
who
can wear me down
first
not knowing

I'd already
been stupid enough
to say yes
once

Ayo! I'm only gon let you call my girl shorty once
aight?
Derek says, with a wink
chucking his sweaty towel at me

wishing he wouldn't
call me that I start to
yell back in protest

but Coach has this stupid
rule where I'm only seen
and not heard until practice is over

says there's only
one coach runnin the team
and it *definitely ain't nobody wearin panties*

so I pretend not to hear
turn my back and ignore
his fake attempts to claim me

Practice somehow ends
a half circle
around the now-full
basket of sweaty towels
set in front of me
the team talking
about
the party

a half circle
of jokes flung
around
amongst players
mapping out
how much ass
would be up for grabs

a half circle
of plans targeting
available fresh meat
how to get it
who could get it
what it took to get it
first

If you want to get first dibs
on a freshman:
you gotta walk up to her
right

walk up to her real smooth
with a cup in your hand
right

cause you know bitches like free shit
feel me
explains Elliot, point guard, in between daps

you walk up to her
tell her you heard all about her
put ya hand on her lower back

like right above her booty
make her think
she the only one in the room

make her think she special
like she the only one you want
right

when she ask what you heard
just tell her you don't believe the hype
just tell her you rather she show you

the truth

Son, that was the corniest shit
I've ever heard
you can't tell me
that actually works

these are college women
they're not falling
for these corny ass lines

talkin about
how you rather they show you
Derek says, winking at me attempting to earn

points

you gotta be too busy
to notice they even there
cause you're busy and shit

then BAM!
slide in the DMs with all the jokes
let em know you not pressed but then have em

laughin
[nope
wrong again]

oh yeah, well
it worked on that shorty
from Brooklyn

Elliot shoots me a look
what's her name again he pauses, snapping his finger
oh yeah

Sophia

I don't know if it's Sophia
coming up in conversation
or Derek being stupid enough
to share his weak game with the team
as if he believes that's how he "got" me
but suddenly the gym is much smaller
than it was before
and the sweat stink
of all the players
becomes my own
coating the insides
of my nostrils
and all of my teeth

well we all
make mistakes sometimes,
don't we I blurt out
louder than planned

the whole team freezes
turning toward the useless thing
they suddenly realize is still standing here listening
and wait for Elliot to respond with something clever

well we all know what it's like
to slide through the campus ho
from time to time
don't we Elliot replies locking eyes with me

in between handshakes

I hear fast steps
between my heavy breaths
coming from behind me
outside
heading far
away from the gym
my fist tightened around
my bunch of keys
each one squeezed
between fingers
just the way I'd learned
on the news
always
ready for attackers
strange men
I don't know
on the street

Derek's life
spared
by the sound
of his voice
calling my name
pulling me alert
just before rushing
to block
my path

Come on, Slim, slow down
it's just me
he says finally catching up

that supposed to mean something?
I cut

well you been in my bed, so—
    don't I cut him off

that's exactly what I'm talking about
you're no different from the rest of them

what, cause I was talkin about women
with the team, come on now he pleads

because you didn't say anything
when Elliot called Sophia a ho

well how do I know she ain't one?
he asks, a stupid smirk infamously growing across his face

because she just isn't! nobody calls YOU a ho
even though all you and those assholes do is talk about is gettin girls

cause women are women and men are men
and they shouldn't be out here tryna do what we do

I told you your mouth was gon get you in trouble
he continues *you don't need to be out here tryna*

save hos like Sophia unless you want people
thinking you're one too he says reaching for my waist

so what if they do think it I say
is the whole world gonna hate me too?

Kendra says I should meet her on the yard
the part of campus
that seems like
the whole school
revolves around it
with old classroom buildings

shaped to its four corners
facing the university flagpole
just in case you ever get lost
amongst the crowds
of all the other confused freshmen

trying to find ways
to their new homes
that now sit on a hill
found in a new universe of
books, parties, and sex

where we all could just go
back to the center

try our best not to panic
stand still and wait

for someone to discover us lost
and claim us as their own

She's sitting on the steps
to the entrance leaning
against the wall as if this dorm is her own

I'm wondering if I got
the time mixed up

or misread the text
telling me where we should meet

she reads this confusion
on my face immediately

I figured I better meet you back here
you know   just in case you

try to climb out the back window
run the other direction or something

by the look on your face
I can tell I'm probably right

It's harder to close out the world
when a whole new one
is sitting there
smiling up at you
waiting at your doorstep

when you notice
she's let her hair down
ditched the tee and sweats
for a crop top and jeans

when you're curious
wanting to know what it's like
to not let the day
rob you of a good night

A thick cloud
thrusts itself
out into the air
at the entrance
of the dark blue
row house we
could already hear
from down the street
as if it'd been waiting
for somebody
to set it free

off-campus housing
apartments
with their own
set of rules
set by upperclassmen
who've earned rights to wreck
eardrums
lungs
liver

damp bodies
so full they tip over
pour out
onto the sidewalk
with the smoke
Kendra pulls me in
before I can
change my mind

In my mind
college parties
were painted
just like this:

everything too loud
everywhere too dark
everyone close and touching

Kendra leads me
to open space
toward the back

we pass by walls
that dudes lean against
not yet drunk enough to dance

talking to girls
not yet drunk enough
if grabbed to go along

reach the kitchen
where everyone surrounds
a table with cups

bottles glisten
being passed and emptied
under dim light

standing behind it
Elliot at the center
a red cup in hand

the other
rested above
a freshman girl's booty

Look who it is
shorty with the smart mouth
always givin somebody
a hard time

what you drinkin tonight
he asks, placing his hands
on the table

leaning over the bottles
his attention fully turned
toward me

you need to loosen up
we all here
to have a good time

my eyes flick down
at the can of soda already in my hands
thanks but I'm good

his smile widens
so I can see how he gets
first dibs in action

then glances at Kendra
eyes scan the full length of her body
from behind the brim of his cup

sips and asks *and what about you*
sweetheart?
don't tell me you scared of a good time

too

It couldn't have been
more than fifteen minutes
since we'd gotten there
but we felt the steady press
of new people at the party
on our backs getting harder
to hear and bodies forced
to move in tight

Kendra takes a step
closer to the table
making sure her eyes
meet with Elliot's
scared for what,
sweetheart?
we're good

besides I bring
my own "good time," she air quotes
who knows how long
you been at this table
running your mouth
or what type of shit
you've done to these drinks

be careful, sis, she warns the girl
still waiting silent behind Elliot
with a paused look
over his right shoulder
grazes my arm
as she turns toward
the music
and walks away

Elliot throws up the Black Power fist
mocking Kendra's solidarity
with his next freshman conquest
laughs to himself
opens his mouth
to say something else to me

I hear nothing now
with my back turned
but the sound
of the music growing
louder above the crowd

see how Kendra
swings her hips
with her eyes closed
lets herself sway
solo to the beat

in just minutes
watch how many hands
of sweaty unknowns she swats
dodging entitled boys' advances
drawn to her free curves

watch her wave off
attention most girls wish for
watch her shoo away
come-ons in the dark attracted
like flies to a dangerous light

She opens her eyes
only for a second
coyly smiles with them
using them
to invite me over

at first I think
to say no
then let my body
take me

Minutes later
the crowd becomes
a circle around me
around us
feeling the music like
every song is mine
every drum kick
bassline connecting
her winding hips
and my thighs moving in and out
we don't notice the crowd thicken
till the dj shouts us out
we still forget
people are looking
feel myself lose it
hearing hip-hop
shift to soca
then become afrobeat
feel rhythms rock
any inhibition
I came with
feel every surface
on me moisten
feel my center
tingle
rise
heat

We're snapped back
into reality when a girl
whose face I can't really see
bumps too hard against me
on her way to the bathroom
a guy who looks familiar
trails close behind her
one hand
on the small
of her back
holding her steady
a familiar wave
of heads turns toward
the shiny figure's
sparkle
beaming both
from her lips
and fingers
covered in rings
I stand still
squint
for a better look
recognize the gloss
the sea of the same
admirers
the dumb smile
charming and ugly
just before
they disappear
behind
a closed door

Are you thirsty
I think I'ma get a drink
it's hot as hell in here
and you were GONE
didn't know
you moved like that
for a second I don't
realize who's
talking to me

huh?

I said it's hot
do you want something
drink? she says
sounding irritated
this time
damn
one minute you here
the next minute you not

Kendra

shit
I'm sorry I—
her hand goes up
motioning me
to stop

fuck em
she reminds me
I'm actually
ready to go, for real
you hungry?

Before Derek and Sophia had walked through
the crowd
it was only me
and Kendra
in that room
sweating
owning the floor
like we were
somebody's
backup dancers
or like
two hot girls
in a cool club
somewhere
in New York City
the sexiest things
under red lights
where everybody
dances consumed
in their own world
before Sophia
barely made it
back there
drunk
in her too-high
heels
before Derek
followed behind her
like a dumb dog
after his bone
it was just us
and I was free

Why didn't you
dance with any
of those guys who
tried to get with you
in there
I ask her coming down
front steps now back outside

they weren't
really tryna dance
Kendra tells me, laughing
with a look that questions
my seriousness and how
I could be so naive

grindin up
on my booty
tryna feel me up
while I dance and they
just stand there
gettin all this for free

that ain't dancing
that's dry humpin
and I'm a—

lady?
I interrupt
attempting
to predict the rest
of her sentence

COLLEGE

•

319

nah   a dancer
I like to actually dance
I don't go to these little parties

to get humped

Both of us
have forgotten the so-called reason
why we left somewhat floating
down the sidewalk just moments
after our waistlines worked up a real appetite

I catch a faint whiff of the jumbo slice spot
just down the street where I know
is tonight's afterparty let-out
the greasy cheese and yeast circles my nose

still not enough to convince me to go in there
where we'd have to deal with the long line
of twisted freshmen leaned up against drunken seniors
fiending to extend their good time

none of it could convince me that all that
would be better than talking to her a little longer
not even the promise of eventual cheap pizza
sounded better than hanging out   just us   right here for a while

We stop at the corner
of Florida and Rhode Island Aves
to wait for the light
Kendra pushes
the crosswalk button
DC has at intersections
as we watch the number
on the light post
across the street
count down

I saw you swattin the flies away too
don't act like I'm weird
for dancing by myself
I just
do my own thing
I see
you like to too
she smiles with a brief
flick of her eyes down my body

the thought of her
watching me
makes my face hot
glad I went to the party
like it was something
I needed
this whole time
but didn't know

Kendra knows the way
back to my dorm by now
without my instructions
walks with me
the whole way home
when she lives
in the opposite direction
makes no big deal
of the time it adds on
to her commute
back to her side of the city
says freshmen
from other states
are safer walking
the streets
with locals by their side
says I should
come to dance class with her
tomorrow morning
to pick up
where we left off

COLLEGE • 323

SEVENTH GRADE

Aunty bends over
a full ninety degrees
pokes her lips out
raises an eyebrow
shakes her butt
side to side faster
than any of the other
black girls I've seen
at school when she dances
to the sounds of "Sweet Mother"
the song I've heard at least

one thousand times
at these Nigerian parties
we go to every other month
blares from the speakers
like clockwork all the women
responsible for the massive spreads of
jollof rice stews and fufu
emerge from the kitchen

marching clapping
shaking their shoulders
winding their hips
move from all sides of this
rented church hall flexing
skills they'd learned as children
grown up in the village
elaborate geles adorn glossy weaves
matched long fabrics tied to waists swinging
this native dress gleams
under bright party lights
all the women dancing
toward and around each other
rhythm of their bodies
moving as one

Aunty extends a hand
stretched with a wave in my direction
an invitation to join her and the other women
in this dance that I always decline

this pride I see spread across their faces
their bodies all familiar with what to do
their eyes scanning themselves in admiration

as if they all know who and what
they come from beyond names and roles
they've been given

witness something bigger
course through their veins
sense a confidence I don't yet think

I can call mine

Tonight is Aunty's last few hours
in America now that it's time to go back home
where her house in Nigeria no longer needs to be
watched by Uncle who has been there
with it alone while she lived with us for a year
I'd begun to hear her on the phone with him
talking more often, saying his name
with a tone that sounded more like love
than what she used months before when
she and I warred over what I was allowed
to do under the new set of rules she'd created
for her Fat American Niece
I liked seeing her smile more like that
tell me stories of when she was a girl
how she *wasn't looking good for no man*
listened as her voice began softening the more
time we spent together alone after the first time
I discovered blood in my panties
a time when she was the only person around
who I could tell

Aunty
always
with attitude
always
pointing with her lips
always
the family gossip
always
a pidgin wordsmith
always
in my things
always
in my face
always
in my heart
always
in my mirror
always
was teaching
me about
my feelings
and moving
me to say
what was
on my mind
Aunty

always a reminder
of fight
of pride

COLLEGE

My phone buzzes early
with Kendra's instructions
to meet her on the corner
of H Street and Thirteenth
tells me I should wear
whatever I want
as long as I can move
tells me not to worry
about paying for class
that she's got me
tells me to be on time
which means
I need to leave
soon

Getting off the bus
I can't ignore all the windows
facing the street where
dancers fill the other side
of the glass
a crowd of them barefoot
gliding across a black floor
cannot make out any faces
glad to know
it'll be hard to be seen

Kendra's favorite dance teacher
talks so much shit that I forget
people pay to take his class willingly
he uses all the names and faces
he knows in the room
happy that I'm not one of them
I learn early to do whatever he says
follow his body if I want
answers to the questions
that pop into my brain
like what comes after this or
what count is next or
what to do with my hands
the few times I scan the room
searching for the one person
I know here and snapped back
into the movements for fear
I'll be called out
despite the fact that he drags
us like dogs unworthy
of his presence or his time
I feel myself find the rhythm
feel myself get lost in the moves
feel my back bend into itself
proud to meet every challenge

see all that I can do
when forced to show up
and get my body in line

His name is Torion
he stands like you could
draw a straight line
from ceiling to floor
along his back

everything about him
sharp bulging curve and upright
always prepared to dance
circles around us

oh and he does

beside our unworthy behinds
his body looks statuesque
like years of hard work
draped in fashionably loose fabric

that keeps catching the air for effect

After leading us through the long warm-up
that everyone in the studio
seems to know but me
we're all damp bodies and
Torion tells us
I need four lines
facing the windows
I'd just walked by outside

tells us
look
to your right and your left
memorize who you've got
to stick with every time
you go across this floor, honey
tells us
no duets and no solos
to listen
to watch
to breathe

Watching Kendra
float across the floor
in unison with her line
of dancers who've
been here before is like
watching a family of free birds

who've created
their own way to fly
glide across a sky
they each use their
arms and legs to slice through

no air no body no steps
too tough to get past
no demands barked loudly
too much for their fierce bodies
to match

no beat too fast
for wings to dive into

I've gotten lost in the beat
when I realize
it's my line's turn
to cross the floor
using the sixteen counts
given to the class
just fifteen minutes ago
my brain tells me
I can't remember
anything I just saw
the lines before us do
over and over
again

I look
to my left
and look
to my right
to see who
I dance with
and see
their bodies
in ready position
then feel the memory
of the steps
return

We go on like this for twenty minutes
going back and forth across the floor
doing things it seems like just popped
into the instructor's head right in front of us

he keeps telling us *you ain't in here by yourself!*
keeps telling us *dance like you know who the fuck you are!*
keeps telling us *y'all better forget about these damn mirrors and*
   feel something!

tells us to listen to our bodies and I don't
know how I'm supposed to do it all at once
but it feels so good to try

The clothes we all came in with
are all now darker versions of themselves
soaked in the salty wetness of the last hour

when I think it's just about over this is when
he tells us that it's time to put it all together

something in me panics wondering what
that means if I didn't sign up to perform

I just showed up to a class to learn
and I know I'm not ready for a test

he teaches some counts that look familiar
the moves we'd done over and over again

across this black floor whose dirt now
thickly coats the bottoms of my worn feet

shows us how the moves are supposed to be done
knowing that none of us can do it like him

my eyes study every inch of his skin
his face his hands his legs his feet

do my best to commit it all to memory
do my best to avoid making a fool

of myself

I don't recognize myself
in this small group he's put me in
with only four of us and me in the middle
all I know is when he turns the music on
I become a slice of someone I'd always wished
I could be

all I know is that I wanted to see
the girl in my reflection keep up for once
see her do the steps like they came
from somewhere
inside

We all thank him
as our soaked bodies
pour out of the studio turned
steam room and I feel
his eyes follow me making
my way up the line
a hint of a smile
he'd fought to force down
during class now
spreads lightly across
his face when he asks me
where I'm from
then tells me *chile,*
you need to be
back in this class
tells me
I know
I better see you
next week

He likes you
if he thought you were trash
he wouldn't have said anything
he would have just shook
your hand and said 'thanks for coming'
Kendra explains

he told me that I NEED to be in class
he basically said I'm terrible
I didn't see him telling you
and your little dancer friends that
I reply

that's because he already
got on my ass years ago
I work and practically live here, remember?
you want that dude to leave you alone?
show up and work

We both reach
for our toes sitting on the ground
outside the studio as the next class
moves through the warm-up

Kendra's advice plays over and over
again in my mind while I exhale
face down across my knees the way she showed me

If I want the instructor off my back
I need to show up

If I want to be good at this
I have to do the work

and the words sound a lot
like my dad's advice

about school

My head spins listening
to the professor talking about credits and debits
cause I still don't know the difference
between its meaning in accounting
and the cards you use to buy things

one of them Dad always taught me
to use if I got the money
the other I use if I'll have it soon
enough to pay it back

before I came here Dad took me
to the bank for my first credit card
seeing my eyes grow big when it finally arrived
warned me to use it only for emergencies

warned me if I must use it to pay it back quick
warned me of the evils of spending money
that I don't have on things
that don't matter

told me
hold tight
to the little
I have

told me
spend only
on things
that matter

I look down again
at this ancient five-hundred-page book
cracked open only on occasion
out of fear of failing

wonder what I'm supposed
to do with it
how I'm supposed to learn
something I hate

    what matters?

Maybe you'd know a little something
if you paid attention sometimes
the professor says on my way out

I was, Professor Gray, I'm always listening
I schmooze the way Dad taught me

if you weren't busy daydreaming you'd know the class laughed
at your question because the girl who raised her hand

right before you already asked the same thing
scholarship students always think

they can just skate their way through
if you want to keep that scholarship money, miss lady

you better get your head in those books
I don't care what those silly high school teachers told you:

stupid questions do exist
you better not keep showing up to my class

proving me right

Professor Gray shakes her head
at me as I walk away
feeling her laser beams
of shame graze my neck
I wonder how I'll survive
class without the books
she claims I need to get in

books   multiple   more than I'm willing to buy

outdated and overpriced
assigned to help us somehow
survive this class and the others
costing an arm and a leg
that I'd rather be using to dance
I glance back over my shoulder

back at Professor Gray and lie:
I won't, Professor
I promise you
I'll get back to it
tonight

Tonight I came here alone
surprised I made it back
without the help
of Kendra's instructions

she doesn't know
I'm here
part of me scared

Torion
won't have her
as distraction

will narrow his eyes
to the new dancer
in the room

who he will
not hesitate to run
to the ground

part of me scared
of the Me
who knows this

and still
comes back
for more

Look who came back for more
I see you must be a masochist
didn't get dragged enough the first time
so you done came back
to have that ass whooped one more time
cause you didn't learn your lesson before
huh?

already he's on me with the threats
of how hard this will be
how hard this will be for me cause I'm new
a big part of me an eternal eye roll
the other warmed by the fact
that he remembers

Masochist (mas·och·ist)
/'mazəkəst,'masəkəst/
noun
a person who enjoys
an activity
that appears
to be painful
or tedious

as in
only masochists
pay twenty dollars (one fifth of an accounting foundations book)
to be called out
repeatedly and told
what needs to be fixed

only masochists
spend two hours
on a monday
studying dancing when they're
in danger of failing
out of their actual major

only masochists
come back to a place
that will leave them
aching
the next morning

leave them
less able to pay
for school books
and love it

There are only seven of us here
so he makes us feel every bit of it
has us do all things over and over
until it is at least a fraction
of his expectations

class is different this time
now the warm-up is something
I've seen before and that I know
is coming

there are only three lines
that go across
with the third one being
just me

every part of my body
quakes deep
from within when
it's my turn to go across

every eye in and out
of this room on me
suddenly a hatred for these mirrors
these large windows

where all can see
this body get it wrong
how obvious it is
that I know nothing

my ears burning hot
with pressure from the inside
his commands coming
from the out

Let me tell you something:
you ain't gonna learn
how to turn without turning
all this pretending and doin it
halfway is gonna
rob you of the chance
to really dance, honey

all this yelling he does
actually makes sense
all of it simple but not easy
I don't know how to make my body
do what it's so afraid of

I don't know how
to try at something
knowing I will fail
seeing the fear in my face
he doesn't give us time to know

he presses play again
then tells us to imagine
something on the ground
tells us to imagine using
our legs and arms
to get around it

There's no way around
the fact that I've never learned
the proper way to turn
I haven't been trained
I only know how to move
my feet to drums by the lead of my hips

I don't know why I'm here
why I've brought myself back
into this room to embarrass myself
why I've signed up to be
exposed

I hear him count me in
the rhythm leaves no space
to stay in my fearful trance

all I know is there are things
on the floor I'm using my body

to get around and to get over
somehow

my body begins to understand
what it really means to turn

I hear him say
feet in fourth position

my legs move placing one foot
in front of the other toes facing out

I hear him say
prep

my arms open with elbows bent
like a hug with only breath in the space

I hear him say
push

my thigh uses my back leg for momentum
letting the front leg lift the heel off the ground

we hear him say
don't forget to spot

to get my body around:
I must use my eyes

to tell it where to go

Before I can tell myself
that I still look like a fool
that I don't belong in this class
with its mirrors all around me
and its music too fast
to keep up

I'm prepping
I'm pushing
I'm spotting
I'm turning

I'm moving across this black floor
Torion slaps his hands together

screams

YES!

Oh my god you shoulda seen me
I don't know I—
I just, like, I just
DID that shit!

I don't even
know how it happened
but before I knew it—

I was turnin all the way
across that floor
and I still don't know

how I did it
but I did and all I know
is I never did that before!

it was just
SO CRAZY cause I didn't
think I could do it

without you there

Kendra's smirk
turns into a full smile
laying across the floor
the way she does
whenever she's
hanging out in my room
listening to me gush
on a high after
another class
without her

I stop ranting
when I admit aloud
how scared I'd been
to go alone
how much better
I feel
when she's around

well it was never
about me, silly
you got the juice
and even though
I can't belieeeeve
you betrayed me like this
she jokes

I'm not surprised at all
this is what happens
when you keep going back
and trying
she pauses

you start learning how to listen
to your body
she pauses, again looking up at me
and your heart

The heart
is deceitful
above all things
and desperately sick;
who can understand it?

Jeremiah 17:9

Who can understand the way
my heart
is thumping
so hard
against the inside
of my chest
so hard
still fighting against
what Kendra
is always saying
I'm surprised
she can't
hear it
surprised
as she stares
that she can't
see my chest
jumping
trying to beat
the truth:
that what's
in my heart
feels
like too much
feels
so good

it's got
to be wrong

I break out
of her gaze
continue my rambling
as I walk
into my bathroom
change
my clothes

come back out
start emptying my bag
spreading my books
trying to change
the subject

pull out the one
accounting textbook of the three
I'm supposed to have
read one sentence

decide I'd rather sleep

There's no wiping the sleep
fully from my eyes
crusted in the corners
of them as I brush past
rows of desks and seats
full way before I arrive

Professor Gray pausing
dramatically as I make
my way to the back
repeats the date of our first exam
three times making sure

to emphasize how much
of our overall grade
it will count for
that begging, pleading
and excuses will get us nothing

if we don't find a way
to study

Yo what is wrong with you girl
you stay missing this class
like you got SO many more
important things to do
don't you wanna pass?
Kelly whispers
as I plop down
in a seat one row
in front of her

you neeever show up
to the study groups
between all of us
we got all the books
we need
stop being dumb
she continues

of course I wanna
pass this stupid class
my dad will kill me
if I don't
I whisper back
I'll come tonight
promise

What is something you need
to overcome?
who are you even dancing for?
Torion asks

he's turned off the music
stopped us mid-class
asking these two questions

that no one here
seems to know
how to answer

hello anybody?
why are you here?
you must know why

you keep coming back here
and if you don't that's probably
why you're in here just flopping around

You
who are you dancing for?
he slows pace
stopping right
in front of me
I'm talking

to you, sis
who are you dancing for?
he pushes, repeating
the question waiting
for me to answer

I-d-don't-I-
this stupid stuttering thing I do
whenever I'm nervous
or know I'm not
being honest

takes over my mouth
when all I want to do
is lift my chin up
look him in the eye
and say:

Me

Well is that how you do it?
he questions
somehow reading my mind

is that how you dance
for yourself?
with your head down
looking at the ground
like you don't know
where you're going
or who you are?
he continues

no
it isn't
I-don't-I don't really
how am I supposed
to know who I am
I don't really know where
I'm going but I'm
trying to figure it out
I whisper low enough
for the class not to hear

but loud enough
to somehow
get help

He looks at me and smiles
even though I feel like I should
just pack all my things and leave

who has time for someone
who's confused

who wants to be around someone
who's always scared

who wants to keep
wasting their breath

on a girl who seems like
all she knows how to do

is try

We're all figuring this out
everybody spread out
find a space in the room
and lay on the floor
I'm gonna put on
some music
and say some things
to you
and I want you
to use this whole room
to do whatever your body
tells you
close your eyes
and listen
to what it
tells you
to do

I can't explain
what happens to me in the next
twenty minutes of class but maybe
I've been possessed by something

back in my father's church sometimes
everyone would watch someone
who they called possessed

lie on the ground twisting and contorting
in ways that the body wouldn't
if something powerful weren't inside it

the pastor would command
the spirit inside the body to leave
would pray to drive the spirit out

and everyone in the sanctuary
would pray against the spirit
with hands stretched out toward

the body crying out
in the name of Jesus
that the spirit would be loosed

and sometimes we'd see the body flip over
and the person's head whip forth while the eyes roll back
the wild spirit would take over   cry out   fight through

Possession (pos·ses·sion)
/pə'zeSHən/
noun
the state of having,
owning, or controlling
something

as in
when I forget about
the mirrors
the windows
the eyes
looking at me
judging me
telling me
what they think
I should do
when I forget about
the fear
of pain
of something coming
soon
to hurt me
I am in possession
of my whole body

my spirit runneth over
it twists
it turns
it cries   out

Outside of class
I am so high
off whatever spirit
I just felt
inside me
I go to the desk
pull out
the debit card
full of
money once
stuffed in
graduation cards
and sign up
to take
one more

10:03 PM
dude you're tripping
9:17 PM

where TF are you
we've been here for two hours
we're not going to wait
all night for you again
9:33 PM

fine it's your grade
not mine
I tried to help
10:03 PM

I'm sorry
I got caught up
something I had to do
gonna have to study
by myself
10:21 PM

Maybe it's the fact
that it's late
that I only have
one of the three books
I need for this stupid class
maybe I haven't
been doing enough
or the fact
that I barely ever
make it on time
or that I'm not
trying hard enough
but whatever
it is
it just seems like
nothing inside
of me
cares about
doing this
nothing inside
of me
wants to study
for something
I hate
everything inside of me
unable to find
enough energy
to fake wanting
to do anything
like this
for the rest
of my life

On my fifth read
of the second sentence in chapter three
credits and debits
my phone buzzes at 11:15 PM
thinking it could only
be Kendra calling me
this late
I jump up
to grab my phone
thankful
for an excuse
to stop
and see
the screen read:

MOM

Mama doesn't know
what credits and debits are either
we laugh at the confusion we both feel
she asks how school is going
asks about my father and if he still
lives in that same house
with the woman
her memory still a phantom thing
I have to keep forgiving
I know to move quickly
through the details
I know not to linger
on the trigger

she squeals happily
hearing how I've found
a few new friends
and a job
so I can get my hair done
sometimes
I can hear the smile
cross her teeth
hearing how I'm
doing it all
without my daddy
proud that

she's got
a college girl now

Girl you know I ain't go to no college
you always been
so much smarter than me
always doin so much
I'm proud of you
babygirl
she says with a chuckle

thanks, Mom
I manage

why you so quiet, girl
you sound like you don't
wanna talk to your mama
or something

no Mom it's cool
I'm tired
got a big test comin up
in a few days
I'm just tired is all
you called so late

oh it's me, of course
she snarls
I'M calling YOU too late
she continues
well WHEN'S THE LAST TIME
YOU CALLED your mama, huh?
I just FIGURED it's been
TOO DAMN LONG

EXCUSE THE HELL
OUT OF ME she finally says
no longer trying to soften
her voice

I was waiting for this mama that I know
this mama I've always got to be
careful with

this mama who is more thorn
than rose petal

this mama always a ticking time bomb
ready to explode

this mama who's missing someone
she always hurts

this mama who wishes I'd just
call sometimes

think of her
some days

remember that
no matter what

it's her that I came from
it's still her that I owe

for the pain

Mom I gotta go
I try to say
gently
trying to cool her down

well of course you do
of course you're too busy

for little old me
she says trying to guilt me

Mom, stop
you called super late

expecting me to just
talk to you all night

it's not like we have a lot
to talk about anyway

and every time we talk
I have to repeat myself

WELL THAT'S FINE DON'T CALL ME
NO MORE THEN she screams

Mom, you called me
stop screaming at me like that

YOU DON'T TELL ME WHAT TO DO
I'M YOUR MOTHER

I'LL SAY WHATEVER THE FUCK
I WA—

Mama calls me back
three more times tonight
leaving two long voice mails
the first one threatening yet
gentler than I know the second
one would be if I chose to listen

I delete both voice mails
turning off my phone for the night
thinking the passing time
had gotten us past this believing
we could talk without it becoming

another fight

Good morning, Mom
I think it's better
if we don't talk
for a while
I don't want
to keep hurting
your feelings
and the things
you say always
hurt me
I love you, Mom
but I need you
to leave me
alone for a while
take care
of yourself
9:44 AM

accounting class
began at 8:00 AM
it's 9:45 AM now
and I'm still
laying here
in this tear-soaked pillow
sending my mother
this text

before I block
her number

What's going on with you?
Kendra breaks the ice
after walking beside me
for ten whole minutes
in silence

I'm just tired is all
I missed class again
and my—I just
I just need sleep

it seems like that's
all you do now besides
take class without me
she says with a smile
jabbing her elbow into my side

she goes silent again
when I don't laugh

look if you don't
wanna hang out with me
anymore it's cool just say it

that's not what it is
it's just that everything—
my phone buzzes
Dad   again
I press ignore

You're ignoring calls from your dad now?
I thought you were Daddy's Little Girl
she tries to joke again

it's probably just another one of his
reminders about how I need to stay focused

look I'll talk to you later
when I get off work

I'm about to be late
I say

Kendra's smile drops and it's like
a basketball's been thrown at my chest

I promise, I—
I just can't talk right now

I mean, it's cool
she says looking off to the side

maybe I'll see you around
in class or something

Something's got to be wrong with me
fifteen minutes late for my shift
Coach's eyes stab me
watching me hurry in
the players run their laps
as I rush to get their towels
and water ready
Derek flashes me
a dumb smile that I ignore
Kendra's defeated smile
flashes across my memory
and I just miss a basketball
that flies by my head
opening my phone screen
to a long text from Dad

call your mom back
she says you hung up on her?
I know how she is
but I didn't raise you like that
you don't hang up
on your mom

love, Dad
4:21 PM

what is with parents
signing the ends of
text messages

who even taught my dad
how to text

There are thirty towels to fold
three water kegs to fill
fifteen jerseys to put in the washer
twelve players' eyes to avoid
while Kendra, school
and my parents flood my mind

today Elliot winks
every time he stops for water
tries to graze my hand
in exchange for a towel
points out my smart mouth

one too many times before
I forget where I am
throwing everything
on the time-out table
at his stupid face

I don't hear the coach's
whistle pausing practice
I don't hear Derek's footsteps
come running toward me

until he's gotten up close asking me
what's going on between us
it's then that I look around at
every eye I'd been trying to avoid
a mess I've made proof

that the problem here is me

***The problem is**
that it ain't nothin goin on
ain't nothin goin on between us
or any other dude
we know y'all don't do
nothin but pretend to study,* Derek
Elliot says to the coach,
but loud enough to be
an announcement
*she gotta issue
every time a dude
even looks at her
your little girlfriend
got a problem with boys
rather shake her ass
at parties with bitches*

Kendra's face flashes
before my eyes
but Derek's body
blocks my ability to lunge
while laughter breaks out
amongst the team

*NOW WHAT IN THE HELL
IS GOIN ON OVER HERE*
Coach asks approaching
out of breath

before I can stop myself
my mouth gets me
into trouble:
Coach, I quit

This time Derek somehow finds a way
to follow me
all the way
back home
where I don't
tell him
to leave
where I don't
tell him
that he needs
to go so I can be
alone
the way
I want

he says
I shouldn't be
all by myself and that
he knows how we
can prove what Elliot said isn't true
(it isn't, right?)
I let him
touch me
his hands
wandering
all over
his mouth
moving against
my neck

his hand lifts
to muffle me
says that
I just need to let him

take my mind
off all of this
says *ain't no way you could like girls when you can have*   *this*

Derek, I have to go study
you need to leave ri-right now
I can't do th—you have to leave
I have to study and I can't
miss another
study group session or
I'll fail

Derek freezes
slowly lifts his eyes to meet mine
like I'm some kind
fool for choosing
books over him

are you serious
right now? yo
what's wrong with you
shorty?
one second you're quitting your job

and now all of a sudden
you gotta go study
you don't even CARE
about that fuckin class!
he's right

yeah well, I'm about
to go like it enough
to not fail my exam
and you're not—
you're not worth me figuring out what happens if I don't go so
         leave please

Kelly can you please tell me
where the study group is?
I know I haven't been showing up
but I know there's another session tonight
and if you could please tell me where it is
I'll be there in fifteen minutes
7:17 PM

                    smh
                    we're in Robeson Hall
                    third floor room 300
                    we'll be here
                    for another
                    hour and a half
                    7:23 PM

The whole group goes quiet
when I get to room 300
Kelly passes me some copies
she's made for the group
tells me I'm lucky that there's extra
cause she doesn't need hers
anymore

I force a smile of gratitude
find a seat amongst all the papers
books, pens, and half-empty
bags of chips and water bottles
feel ashamed that I've arrived
with nothing to offer

Thirty minutes later
I've gotten nowhere
I stand and grab my bag

announce

that I've got to go
that I can't do this

tell Kelly *I'm sorry*
for wasting your time

she eyes me and my backpack in silence
watches me push my arms through its straps

both of us relieved I'm finally being honest
and deciding not to look back

To a random person

a dance studio // is nothing // but a room with funny floors //
that kind of spring // when you jump on them // funny floors
that sometimes you gotta take your shoes off // to move on //
a random person who's never danced in one before // might
not understand // all these mirrors // all this space // or that
these four walls // are something more // than just a room //
that bodies make things up in // might not understand counts
// or how to let the beat guide you // how to let it speak all the
words you don't have today // today it lets me cry in it // for
the first time in months // in a room all by myself // I don't
have to be // anything // but this // I don't have to explain //
everything I hear // everything I feel // everything I am // is
mine

what is something you need to overcome // who are you dancing for
// what is something you need to overcome // who are you dancing
for // who are you dancing for // who are you dancing for // then
dance like she's here // she's here, sis // dance for her // like this is
your last chance // like it's the last time

Just before running away
that first day I found Kendra here part of me memorized
this room I know where everything is I know how to turn on
the music I walk across the mirrored space slow slow slow
hearing only my stride in it pull out my phone to connect it
turn up the volume it's time to press play slide off my sweats
my hoodie baring my body body body till it's just me in my
sports bra and shorts walk back across the floor and make sure
the door is locked the beat builds builds builds I remember
everything how Torion told me start with my body on the
floor I close my eyes I feel myself myself myself breathing
nothing but my own air begin to pulse I stretch as if to reach
every corner of this floor see the wall touch the ceiling use my
elbows my feet my knees my waist I'm a puppet I'm a doll I'm
a robot I'm a breeze I'm a wave I'm a stopwatch imagining
myself as all things I am all things possible possible possible as
the music fades in and out my limbs stretch contort all about
this room soon I'm animal unable to stop making something
something someone out of all this nothing I am sweat and
growing heat all over having no idea what I'm doing but I'm
here

I've never taken this class before
but I know that Kendra will be here
right now Kelly and everyone else
in accounting have piled into class
taking our first exam that I'll miss

I was already late when I woke up
I've woken up every day since entering
this program hating myself on days
that began there

all I can do is stare
when Kendra walks into the studio
clearly surprised to find me here
before her   stretching

she takes off her shoes
puts down her bag
walks over to sit down next to me
asks me what I'm doing here

what I want
finally

There are fifteen minutes left of class
when the instructor counts us off by six // this means we'll
go in groups // doing her choreography // I realize I didn't
think about this class // being hard // before I came // I just
wanted to dance // I just wanted // to see her // just wanted //
to go somewhere I knew someone would see me // show me
new ways // to be myself // now we're going in groups of six
// suddenly my palms are sweaty // knowing everybody here
// will see me // how ready am I for them to see me // for real
// Kendra squeezes my hand // nudges the small of my back
gently // with the palm of her hand // tells me
just go

It goes so fast
it's over
before I even
have enough
time to be
scared

the instructor points
to Kendra and me
says *again*
says *one more time*
tells the class

    a lot of the time
    the magic happens
    on the dance floor
    when we least expect it
    when we stop doing steps   let go   and dance

    you're never just
    doing steps by yourself in here
    all of you have something special
    a certain kind of magic inside you
    let's celebrate some of that magic we saw today

everybody come
sit in front
give it up
for these
beautiful dancers

And Magic got her name
from the dancing women I saw at church
and from the ones I never saw anywhere
   else
a girl who looks like me
but is strong and does what she wants
is either invisible
or magic

Magic is getting it
all from me

The next morning
the line inside the administration building
is long
stretched outside the add/drop offices
I can't see how many other students
wait to be helped before me with
several seats leading into the hallway
with windows where we
come to submit papers
to pay tuition
drop classes
change majors
abandon our
original plans

my hands tremble holding forms
filled out and signed
to leave what everyone
thought I'd be
behind
they told me
there was a big world
in here
they warned me
of changing my mind
and I knew nothing
but these
buildings
but these classes
but these rules
where I'd come
only as a girl
with instructions and big eyes
but now I know something

about myself
and where my heart
is leading me
so how hard can dreaming really be

My phone rings on the way out of the admin building
see the screen read DAD
and answer this time
think to make up
some elaborate lie
to explain why
I haven't been
answering his calls
or some explanation
about why college
has been so tough
for me

instead I stand still
ask him to listen
tell him
something's changed
tell myself

to breathe

Acknowledgments

It takes a whole village to write a book and I wouldn't have written this one if it hadn't been for the people who believed in me enough to tell me to try.

Jason Reynolds—when we met twelve years ago I didn't even know that I wanted to do this writing thing for real. And you smiled all big and called yourself a writer with no "and." When I didn't know anybody else our age who looked like us could do it big you told me it was possible and that I could do it my way. Thank you for being the best mentor I could ever ask for and, even more so, for being one of my best friends. You been looking out this whole time. Thank you for telling me to give this thing a real shot. Thank you for seeing me before many others did. I love you, friend. I almost gave up several times and you told me how unfortunate that would be. I am beyond grateful. You still corny, though. I hope this makes you cry and WHEN you do there's people that owe me money.

Shout-outs to my long-standing writing communities. The spaces that gave my work early wings and space to grow: SPIT DAT open mic, VONA, and Rhode Island Writer's Colony. The Magic Six: Axie, Gaby, Stephanie, Devon, and Michelle. There's seriously no match for the room to work out your ideas with supportive writers/listeners/community.

To Sasha Jackson, for encouraging me to write my very first poem that one night in our study group at Howard University.

Big love to my teachers throughout this process who taught me how to cut what wasn't necessary while still finding ways to tell the whole story: Tracey Baptiste, Adrian Matejka, Ruth Forman, Tony Medina, Cathy Park Hong, and again, Jason Reynolds. There's nothing like cutthroat feedback to send a little sensitive baby like me into tears but then back to the page. Thank y'all for telling me the truth.

Thank you to Hi-ARTS, Alexandria Johnson, Asante Amin,

Najee Ritter, Kirya Traber, Chukwumaa, and Lacresha Berry for believing in this story when it still was a rough draft and a one-person stage play. Y'all made my first dreams come true by helping me bring its early skeleton to life.

Sasha Banks. Asha Santee. You both have been a big part of why I haven't given up throughout this process. The random check-ins. The FaceTime dates. The visits and sharing of our work. Sibling-hood is important and y'all have both held me so damn tight. My gratitude is endless.

Jacqueline Woodson. *Brown Girl Dreaming* was the first book to . even make me believe I could ever create something like this. And all the work you'd done before I even considered becoming a writer inspired me more than I have words for. Thank you for reading my work and finding it worthy of your kind words. I hope I make you proud.

My Howard University Fam—I just want to say I love you for changing me in ways that I needed most. I needed to experience life as a black person away from home in a world that would affirm all of me and y'all really did that for me. My experience on our alma mater's campus is what helped birth this story and helped it come full circle. We had our reasons for choosing an HBCU and I will never regret doing so. May we always support each other's dreams and self-actualization.

To my students of Harlem Children's Zone and Bronx Acad-emy of Letters. My workshop participants at Crossroads, Horizon, and Rikers Island: I love you. Being young and passionate is hard. The world tries to make you small when what you feel and experi-ence is so big. Many of you read my work without even knowing it (surprise!) and gave me the most important feedback. I hope you felt seen somewhere here in this story and the stories to come. Y'all are my greatest muse. I am always thinking about you and carrying you with me.

To Patricia Nelson, my agent. And Andrew Karre, my editor. I am so grateful to you both for supporting my process and never standing in the way of what this story needed to be. You never once tried to silence or sanitize my voice. Thank you for seeing what I've been trying to do and doing all you can to make it possible.

For my Dad: Thank you for instilling determination, bravery, and perseverance in me a long time ago. Those three things have carried me far and kept me pushing no matter where we've disagreed or what resistance I've faced in my journey to becoming an artist. Even when you didn't understand what I'd decided to do with my life, what you'd taught me at a young age helped me have the courage to do what I wanted to do anyway. Thank you for loving me and being there.

For my Mom: Your life taught me a lot about people and how to see people who weren't like me. Even in your death I remember who you were and I see remnants of that fire in myself every time I look in the mirror. I hope wherever you are now, you are living your dreams in peace, too.

And thank you, Reader. Supporter. Community. Fellow Artist. Friend. Your being gives me every reason to keep creating toward the bold, brave healing I want to see in our childhood selves. Thank you for constantly reminding me of the kids in all of us who just want to be felt, heard, seen, loved, and supported.

I love you. Thank you.